HORMONES, HOMICIDES, AND HEXES

North of Forty

Book 2

Lisa Bouchard

Editor: Kathryn Barnsley, KRB Editorial

Cover Designer: Karen Dimmick, Arcane Covers

https://LisaBouchard.com

For Paul, who supports all my dreams.

Table of Contents

ABOUT THIS BOOK

A storm of secrets, betrayal, and peril brews on Shadow Island as private investigator Rebecca Wright faces her most treacherous case yet.

When Rebecca's detestable ex-husband arrives from Boston with his new family in tow, demanding a financial reckoning, her world is thrown into chaos. But personal drama takes a backseat when tragedy strikes: her best friend's uncle is brutally murdered on the island's windswept beach. With her friend consumed by grief, it's up to Rebecca to untangle the deadly web and bring the killer to justice.

As the island's secrets come to light, Rebecca must confront her own past and the dangerous love she thought she'd left behind. With the clock ticking and a heart-stopping chase through Shadow Island's darkest alleys,

Rebecca must unmask the killer before it's too late.

CHAPTER 1

Waking up to find exactly what you needed set out and ready for you was the best feeling in the world. No wonder people used to hire maids and valets.

I pulled on my bathrobe and padded into the kitchen to find a freshly made mug of coffee waiting for me, the Shadow Island Gazette folded next to it. I picked both up and sat in my living room, looking out the window and down at the town center. My first sip of coffee was hot, not too sweet, and exactly what I needed after a night of catching up with Marge and Ellie at the Pickled Seahorse.

It was good to have friends again. The kind of friends who love you no matter what and who are as happy with your success as their own. I thought I had friends in Boston, but I didn't. We were all too busy jockeying to be chair of the next big fundraiser, president of next year's PTA, DAR, or any other three-letter acronym group to care about each other. I'd been on the island for about a year, and it felt like Boston was a world, and a lifetime, away.

I'd settled into my telepathy—practiced using and not using it, until I thought I'd collapse from the mental exhaustion. Running on the beach helped. At five thirty on a misty morning, no one was there and I could let my mental shields down.

I finished my coffee and glanced at the headline of today's paper. Tourists Invade Island.

I frowned. It wasn't nearly that bad. Sure, more tourists were coming to the island because the Maine Steamship Authority ran more boats to it. We were one of the last islands that hadn't turned into a tourist attraction. We had a hotel, lovely beaches, and a few restaurants, but there was nothing special about Shadow Island.

Well, there was. We just didn't tell anyone about it.

Something about the island granted supernatural powers to its inhabitants. Not everyone had powers, but most of us did. My parents were desperate to give me a normal life, so they sent me to college and contrived to make sure I never set foot on the island once I'd left. Too little, too late though. Instead, I was left with a crippling illness, telepathic powers, and the fear I was losing my mind because they never told me what could happen.

It had taken me a while to see their side of the story. My father was a vampire, and he didn't want that for me. My mother had no power at all and didn't want me to feel as worthless as she did. Sending me away, they reasoned, would protect me from everything they were afraid would happen. I finally understood how they felt when my daughter Kelsey asked to come visit. I had a moment of panic before I told her not to take all that time to travel on her break, and that I'd go to her instead.

I still hadn't decided whether I ought to let her on the island or not. That was a question for another day, though. She was too busy at school to think about flying in from California.

I flipped the paper to the police blotter. At first, it seemed like the usual small complaints: a missing bicycle, a noise complaint by the school, and a littering citation. But then I saw a house was broken into. Other than the murders of Angela and Evan Stone, there was practically no real crime on the island.

A gentle chime rang out from my phone. Time to get dressed and head out for my run.

Birds chirped their morning songs as they woke. Waves crashed on the beach, and I breathed in the moist air and let my body settle into the rhythm of the run. Jack and I had no open cases, so the morning would be taken up with training and the afternoon with research. The physical and mental training were tough, but I'd progressed enough that he said he wouldn't want to meet me in a dark alley, or try to hide a secret from me.

The funny thing was, he could hide all his secrets from me because I couldn't see into his mind. Jack wasn't human and, just like the wildlife and pets on the island, I couldn't read his thoughts. I'd tried. I tried when he wasn't paying attention, I tried when he was asleep at his desk, I even tried one night at a bar when he'd been drinking, but there was nothing I could do to get into his head. It was probably for the best—I'm not sure I wanted to know how the fae thought.

Back in my apartment after three miles, I smelled bacon and scrambled eggs waiting for me in the kitchen. I hesitated at the door, trying to decide which I wanted first—food or a shower. The shower won, because I knew my breakfast would stay warm no matter how long I let it sit. Having a magical apartment was the best of the many benefits of my job.

Showered, changed, and fed, I headed downstairs to the office of Jack Magus, Private Investigator.

The outer office had taken on a more welcoming atmosphere now that Abby was our secretary. She'd put a plant on almost every flat surface in the room and hung two bright paintings she'd made one weekend. "Just for fun," she told me when I helped her hang them up.

Just for fun my ass. They were gorgeous impressionistic flowers on large canvasses, and I was impressed that she could do so much with a baby and husband at home. I didn't read her thoughts to see if she was telling me the truth.

She knew what my power was, so why bother to lie? She didn't know that I liked to keep some distance between myself and the people I saw most often.

I studied art in college but wasn't able to create when Kelsey was young. I always felt like I was barely keeping up, and my ex-husband, George, was always ready to let me know when I'd dropped the ball on something.

I walked into the empty inner office. "What a jerk," I muttered, still angry at my ex, but angrier at myself for how I allowed him to treat me. Some days I thought I should be kind to him, for Kelsey's sake. But then he'd do something like send me the birth announcement for his twins. I burned it. Kelsey could keep her relationship with him on her own. I was living my best life far away from him, Chloe, and their twins, Blake and Bryson.

If thinking of them as Beavis and Butt-head in my mind was wrong, I didn't want to be right.

I made a pot of coffee and started reading my way through the Gazette. I was just turning to page seven when there was a knock at the outer door. I opened it to see my friend Marge and her uncle, Randy. Marge looked exasperated and Randy looked like he wanted to be anywhere else but here. "Come on in."

Randy looked around the outer office. "Looks like you're not open yet. We can come back later."

Marge put her hand on his back and pushed him toward the inner office door. "You promised."

I flashed Randy a reassuring smile. "Why don't we talk in my office. No strings—if Jack and I can help, I'll tell you. And if we can't, I'll point you to who can."

I'd do just about anything for my friend Marge or her uncle. Randy was her last living relative except for her husband and children, and he was a great guy. He always seemed to be in exactly the right place when we needed him as kids, and he had a way of talking our parents out of any serious punishments for the wild things we did.

He and Marge followed me into my office, where I offered them coffee but they declined. "Why don't you start by telling me what's wrong."

Randy pursed his lips and scowled, so Marge started talking. "The cottages have been broken into. Mine's been broken into twice. Nothing was taken either time, but I can't keep wondering if someone's going to be there when I get home."

"Since when do you live in a cottage? What about Pete and the kids," I asked.

Her shoulders tensed. "It's only been a few days. I wasn't ready to tell anyone until now. After all these years together, you'd think he'd know better than to get on my last nerve. But no, he had to push me one too many times, so I left."

She and Pete had fought a lot when we were younger, but I thought they'd grown out of it. Apparently not. "And the kids? They're not in the cottage with you, are they?" While lovely, the cottages were designed for one person.

"They're staying with my parents. I need the time alone to decide what I want to do. I was lucky there was an empty cottage, or else I'd be with my parents too."

I reached out and took her hand. "You let me know what I can do to help."

Randy cleared his throat, reminding us of the business at hand.

"What does Connor have to say about the break-ins?" I asked.

"I don't want Connor involved. I can't afford to have the island think it's not safe to live on the beach. The only reason I agreed to talk to you was Marge promised you'd be discreet," Randy said.

Great. Now I needed to keep secrets from the island's chief of police, and my sometime boyfriend. Good thing I was the telepath in the relationship. I took out a notepad and started writing.

"All of the cottages have been broken into?" I asked.

"Yes. As far as I know, only mine was twice," Marge said.

"And last night, they spray-painted graffiti on every cottage," Randy added.

I found it hard to believe none of the tenants had talked to Connor. "You're sure no one's gone to the police yet?"

Randy frowned. "Had to offer them a hundred dollars off their rent to let me take care of it."

I reached into my desk drawer, pulled out a contract, and handed it to Randy. "I tell you what, Jack and I will look into this for you. We'll do what we can, but eventually news of this is going to come out."

Randy signed the contract without reading it. "I know, but if it's secret until after you catch the guy, that'll be fine."

"Okay then, we'll start right after you pay our retainer."

He looked confused. "Retainer? What retainer?"

I handed him the contract back. "Maybe you should read this."

Both he and Marge read the contract. He handed it back again, this time with a check. I'm not sure he read the fine print carefully, because he didn't ask about having his thoughts read.

"Who do you think is behind the break-ins?" I asked.

"I don't know. Maybe kids just getting into trouble," he said.

In his mind, I saw a couple high school aged kids that I didn't recognize. I could look them up in the yearbook, though. That was another benefit of living and working on the island, it was easy to find anyone you needed to.

"Okay. We'll start with that angle." I turned to Marge. "Do you keep anything valuable in your cottage? Anything worth stealing?"

"My laptop was there, my flat screen, but no one touched either," Marge said.

A flat screen TV would be too obvious for people to walk out with. A laptop would be easier, but then they'd have to deal with the password protection. If the thief was really a teen, they might not want to bother. "How about jewelry? Anything small like that missing?" I asked.

"I don't have anything particularly valuable except this." She pulled a gold necklace from under her shirt and showed the diamond charm. "I wear it pretty much every day."

"Do me a favor, don't take it off until after we catch the guy."

The outer door opened and Jack and Abby walked in, laughing. Abby put her purse in her desk drawer. "I'll have to try that the next time she won't sleep."

Jack was giving out parenting advice? He had no kids, and although he was raised by human parents, he wasn't even human. I shook my head and got back to Marge and Randy. "I'll fill Jack in and we'll get to work."

We stood and hugged. I was worried for Marge and hoped she'd be safe in her cottage. "Marge, do you want to stay with me until we get this sorted out?"

She shook her head. "No. Thanks though. I need to think things through on my own."

Jack held the door for Marge, wished them both a good morning, then closed the door.

"New client, Mr. Magus." I said, leaning against the doorframe to the inner office. "His cottages out on the beach have had some break-ins and graffiti. He thinks it's kids being a nuisance. I'm not sure, because it looks like nothing's been taken, at least not from Marge."

Jack smiled. "I was getting bored without a case. Let me guess, he doesn't want to go to Connor because it's bad for business. What was he thinking? And did you go through the new client procedure?"

We walked back into the office. This was the first case I'd taken without his help and I wanted to make sure I got everything right. "I've got a check and a signed contract. He thinks it's probably bored high school kids."

He poured himself a cup of coffee. “How about Marge?”

I frowned. “I don’t want to read her thoughts unless I have to. Let’s give it a day or two and see what we come up with.”

He sat at his desk and took a sip of coffee. “At some point you’ll need to get over that. You’ve connected with a lot of old friends, and I’m sure you don’t want to read any of them either. However, if it’s necessary you’ll need to, no matter how you feel about it.”

He was right, but that didn’t mean I had to like it. There must be a superhero movie to back me up on this, right?

Abby called from the outer office. “Rebecca, you’ve got a call. He says he’s your ex-husband. Do you want to take it, or should I take a message?”

My heart sank. I’d been avoiding George’s calls for weeks. He never called about Kelsey and there was nothing else I wanted to talk to him about. "Take a message, please. And don't let him be a jerk to you. If he is, you can hang up on him and I'll buy you lunch."

She chuckled as she took him off hold. "I'm sorry, Miss Wright is out of the office. If you'd like to leave a message, I'll make sure she gets it as soon as she returns."

I could hear his voice growing louder until Abby interrupted him. "Yes, sir. I'll make sure she gets the message."

She walked into the office and wrinkled her nose. "I don't like to judge, but—"

"I claim youth and stupidity. At least now I know better. What did he want?"

"He says since you won't return his calls that he will be here later on this week to force you to speak to him."

I raised my eyebrow. "Force?"

"That's exactly what he said. Force."

I sighed. If I'd wanted to talk to him, I'd have returned one of his many calls. "It's a four-hour drive, and he'll have to time it right to catch the ferry. I doubt he'll make it here, it's too much effort. And I can't imagine what he wants to talk to me about."

"I don't like the sound of this. I should call him and find out what he wants," Jack said.

"I can't have my boss running interference for me. I'll call him tonight and see if we can't settle whatever his issue is over the phone."

"Yes, but as your attorney, I should handle things related to your divorce. Don't agree to anything over the phone and demand he comes here to settle the issue. As you said, he probably won't show up. But if he does, we'll meet here, and Abby can put Connor on standby because I don't trust your ex."

I took my car to the Gazette office to talk to Marge. I didn't ask her, or her uncle, everything I wanted to because people sometimes answer differently if they're together.

Her office was fairly quiet. Marge looked up and smiled at me when I opened the door. "Thought you'd come by sometime today."

I looked around. The office had several people working at their desks. If Randy wanted these break-ins to be kept secret, discussing them in front of the town's reporters was not a good idea. "Is there somewhere we can talk privately?"

Marge pressed a few buttons on her phone. "Conference room is empty, and I can answer the phone from there now."

I followed her and we both sat after I closed the conference room door. The room held an oval table with eight leather chairs around it, a complicated phone used for conference calls, and a short storage cabinet with pens, notepads, and bottled water on top of it.

She clasped her hands and rested them on the table. “Thanks for doing this, Becks. I know it’s a lot to ask you not to tell Connor, and Uncle Randy and I appreciate it.”

I nodded. “Like I said, if I think I have to, I’ll turn the investigation over to him. But if it’s just a routine B&E and some graffiti, I won’t need to until we capture your guy.” I took my notepad from my bag. “I just want to confirm that nothing was taken from your cottage.”

She shook her head. “No. Nothing. That’s the weird thing. Why keep coming back if you’re not going to take anything?”

I shrugged. “It definitely sounds like kids just getting into trouble. But Jack and I will investigate, to make sure. In the meantime, your uncle should consider extra security.”

“I thought about that, but if they’re not taking anything, I don’t want to make it harder for them to get in.”

I squinted at her in confusion. What on earth was she talking about?

"You know, if they can't get in, they may break the door down and then I'd have to get it fixed. Right now it's kind of a no-harm-no-foul situation."

I sighed. Maybe I'd spent too much time off the island. "That's not . . ." How could I best describe this to her in a way that she'd take me seriously, but not freak out? "That's not how most crime happens. People escalate until they get caught. The sooner they're caught, the safer you'll be. Whoever broke in tried not to leave any trace, but later on, they moved to graffiti, demanding things of you. I promise that kind of escalation will lead to a lot more trouble."

She frowned. "I suppose you're right. But I can't help thinking that it's someone I know. I mean, it must be. No one's going to come from the mainland just to break into our cottages. I don't want them to get into any real trouble, you know."

"I guess I thought you'd be more jaded by now, working at the paper."

She took a bottle of water from the cabinet and raised an eyebrow at me. I held my hand out and took the bottle. "Nah, all I do is answer the phones. The reporters might be more jaded, but honestly, you know this town. Other than that double murder that you solved, there's basically no crime."

I wasn't sure about that. If there wasn't any crime, why did the town have both a police force and a private investigator's office? "Who are your uncle's other tenants?"

"Lulu Sandoz is in the first cottage, I'm in the second, Janet Cosgrave is in the third, and Mamie Knight is in the fourth," Marge answered.

I didn't know Lulu or Janet well, but I'd known Mamie all my life. She had to be at least a hundred years old. "Mamie? She's still living on her own?"

"She is. Won't let anyone talk her into moving either."

I doodled on my notebook as we talked. "Not even with the break-ins?"

Marge laughed. "No. She's the least bothered. She says it's going to take more than some young punk to drive her out of her home."

I wrote *young punk* on my notepad. "Why young? Did she get a look him?"

She opened her water bottle and took a sip. "She didn't say. But at a hundred, everyone's a young punk to you."

Probably true. "I'm going out there next. Can I borrow your key? I'd like to take a look inside and out. Hopefully our young punk left a clue or two for me."

The conference room phone rang. She looked at the caller ID. "I've got to get this. Call me later and we can get together for dinner." She picked up the phone while reaching into her pocket. "Shadow Island Gazette. How may I direct your call?" She handed me her key, already off the ring as though she had anticipated my request.

CHAPTER 2

I put thoughts of Randy's break-ins, Marge's marriage, and my ex aside for the afternoon to attend the funeral of Herbert Krawczyk. Herbert wasn't the kind of man that naturally drew people to him, but he was a Shadow Islander and everyone who was able to attend his funeral did.

One thing that was different about Shadow Island that I never realized until I moved to Boston was that we weren't a religious group. There was one church on the island, but not many people went to services, and it served as more of a community center and social club than anything else. Pastor Bob, having grown up on the island, knew what he was getting into when he was ordained and knew he would only be needed for lifecycle events—baptisms, weddings, and funerals.

Jack and I stood at the edge of the crowd, allowing people who knew the deceased better than we did to move forward. Marge joined us when her husband arrived. He started to walk toward us, but I glared at him and he veered off to stand on his own. Early November wind whipped through the crowd, and I was sure I wasn't the only one hoping to get out of the cold quickly.

"We therefore commit the body of our brother Herbert to the ground. Earth to earth, ashes to ashes, dust to dust; in sure and certain hope of the resurrection to eternal life." Pastor Bob paused and scanned the crowd. "At this time, the family would welcome your remembrances of Herbert."

No one came forward for a full minute. I struggled to come up with one pleasant memory involving Herbert, but nothing came to mind. He'd always been a grouchy old man, yelling at children to be quiet and to leave him alone. I couldn't think of anything I wanted to share about him, and apparently neither could anyone else.

Pastor Bob gave the nod and Herbert's casket was lowered into the ground. "Please join us for Herbert's Celebration of Life in the church's function room."

Marge turned to look at me. "Are you going?" she whispered.

I shrugged. I had a lot of work to do and I didn't have a lot to say to Herbert's family.

"Ian is catering it."

I had an instant change of heart. If Ian was cooking, I wasn't going to miss out.

The celebration of life started out somberly, as we filed into the church's function hall. If Herbert had been a well-loved man, I'd say we were all reliving our memories of him. Since he wasn't, I thought no one wanted to be the first person to break the solemnity of the occasion.

Marge, Jack, and I set our coats down at a table, claiming it as ours. As more people trickled in, they'd look at whose coat was where and choose the table they wanted to sit at. At the front of the room, Ian had set out a simple buffet. Cold sandwiches, salad, and a pasta with spicy-smelling tomato sauce. Cookies, coffee, and tea were on a side table under the window looking out at the cemetery.

We waited for Pastor Bob to arrive, because he would say grace before we served ourselves.

"Did Herbert have many friends on the island?" I asked Marge. I assumed she'd know because she worked at the paper and always seemed to know everything about everyone.

She shrugged. "He's got a few family members on the island, but most people stay out of his way. I don't recall seeing him around town much these past few years either."

Ellie joined us. "Such a sad day."

I nodded somberly. "Did he go into the Horse very often?" I asked, using the town's nickname for our local bar, the Pickled Seahorse.

Ellie's eyes widened. "No. He was banned for six months last year after picking fights with the bartenders several nights in a row. One Friday night Bruce was there and he'd finally had enough, saying his staff didn't deserve to be yelled at."

Bruce Morrigan. That was a name I hadn't heard in ages. He was a year ahead of us in school and did his best to make me forget about Connor. For the few times we'd gone to the Horse since I'd come back to the island, I'd never seen him there.

Pastor Bob and Adam Krawczyk were the last to arrive. Adam's red eyes told us all he broke down once we'd left the cemetery. I didn't know Adam well, he was closer to my parents' age, but it always tugged at my heart to see a stoic man cry. Pastor Bob walked Adam to a table and got him seated, then walked to the front of the room.

We all quieted down, knowing what was coming next. "Let us pray," he said.

"Heavenly father, we pray for the soul of Herbert and ask that you receive him in heaven. We thank you for this food we are about to eat and for the fellowship that will help heal our sorrow. Amen."

Pastor Bob knew his audience—none of us wanted to wait long to eat.

Connor joined our table and gave my hand a squeeze. "You look good in black," he whispered in my ear.

I did my best not to smile. "Thanks." Any urge to smile faded as my mother walked into the room and made a beeline for our table.

"Mind if I join you?" she asked.

I wanted to say no, but I didn't. We hadn't worked out our issues, and I'd been staying away from my parents because I wasn't in the right frame of mind to discuss my issues with them. I didn't want to explain how much the secrets she'd kept had hurt me, or how betrayed I felt when she continued to tell me I should reconcile with George. Instead, I looked away.

"Of course, Mrs. Wright. Why don't you sit here," Jack said, offering her his seat and moving so he was between her and me.

She took her coat off and put her purse on the table. "Doesn't smell like the usual potluck."

Ellie, who was seated next to my mother, smiled at her. It was good to have friends take the pressure off. "Ian's doing the food. Why don't we go up now so we don't miss any of the good stuff."

Everyone from the table followed Ellie and my mother, with Connor and me bringing up the rear. "You're going to have to talk to her someday," he said.

I sighed. "I know. Give me a few more days." I knew I could speak to her if I needed, but I really wanted to enjoy not arguing with her for as long as possible.

Ian supervised the buffet line and winked at me as I approached him. "Your brother's flirting with me," I told Connor.

Connor scoffed. "You and every other beautiful woman on the island."

I swatted his shoulder. "Shouldn't you be defending my honor or some other male bs?"

He handed me a plate. "No. You'll do what you want, and it's my job to make sure you want me."

He was doing a good job of that. We'd spent as much time together as we could, given the constraints of our jobs. Most nights it seemed like one of us, if not both, had a case we needed to work on. Our days weren't any better either. "Are you free tonight?"

He picked up the salad tongs and looked at me. I nodded and he put salad on my plate. "No. I'm still working on the Haskins robbery."

"Still?" Gene Haskins, the mayor of the island, had his house broken into but couldn't locate anything stolen, and I wondered if Connor's case was related to mine. But I couldn't ask, because Randy didn't want the police involved. It would be a lot easier if I could compare anything I found with Connor's case, but I'd have to figure it out the hard way.

Connor put pasta and sauce on my plate, then his. "Every night this week he's got me up there, going through rooms with him, searching for anything missing. So far, nothing. I'm giving him two more days before I call it quits. Boss or not, I can't spend more time looking for nothing."

The mood of the room lightened as people returned to their tables and began to eat. Adam stood and tried to bang his spoon on his glass, but they were both plastic and most people didn't pay any attention to him. Pastor Bob stood and cleared his throat. "I believe Adam has a few words he'd like to say."

Adam turned to the pastor and leaned forward. The woman sitting next to Adam put her arm on his and kept him from falling onto the table. Was this grief or had someone at that table brought a flask? "Thank you," Adam slurred before he turned to face the rest of the room. "Thank you all for being here for my uncle. He was such a good man . . ." Adam trailed off, thinking for a moment. "And I wish I'd spent more time with him, especially lately. But I was busy and kept putting him off."

From my peripheral vision, I could see my mother staring at me. I couldn't keep up the silent treatment for much longer.

"So I hope that any of you who talked to him in his final days would tell me about it. What you talked about, how he was feeling, anything that would give me a better idea of how his last days were. Thank you." He fell back into his chair and closed his eyes.

I looked at Marge and Ellie. "I hadn't seen him at all since I got back to the island. Did either of you?"

Marge pursed her lips. "No. Not that I can remember. And I know I didn't talk to him."

"He was at the Horse two weeks ago," Ellie said. "He was in a great mood, even though he seemed sick to me." She looked over to Adam. "I should go tell him. Maybe he'll feel a little better knowing his uncle was happy up to the end."

"And I should go help Lulu and Mamie. I don't think Janet can handle them herself," Marge said.

I looked to the table where the other three women who lived in Randy's cottages were seated. Lulu and Mamie had probably known Herbert his entire life. I wondered why they didn't have anything to say about him.

Ellie and Marge left the table and my mother frowned. "Not sure what he had to be happy about, living in that old, run-down house of his. And now we know his family didn't talk to him much either. He should have been miserable."

"Mother!" I exclaimed before I could censor myself. "What a terrible thing to say. Some people like to be alone, you know, and everyone's version of happiness is different."

"Don't I know that. Some people throw away a perfectly good life—the life their parents dream they'd have—for some tiny issues," she said, not even trying to hide her anger.

"Okay ladies, let's go outside before we disturb the bereaved."

I looked at him, hoping he'd see how much I did not want to have it out with my mother in the church's parking lot. My mother, on the other hand, smiled. "You're right, Jack. Let's get some air, Rebecca."

Great. I could go quietly with her or risk a scene. "Fine," I said as I stood up. "But I have to get back to work in a few minutes, so this will have to be quick."

We walked outside and I was grateful Jack didn't contradict my lie. I hoped he took my hint and came looking for me in five minutes too. "I know you're not happy with my life choices, but they're mine to make. What you call a tiny issue is actually a breathtaking betrayal that honestly, most people are unwilling to forgive."

My mother scoffed. "I know it's fashionable to say that men can control themselves, but that's never been true. Men will do what they want, and putting up with it is the price women pay for the security of a home for themselves and their children."

I couldn't speak. I just stared at her, unable to believe she thought this was true. "But he left me. He took the security of the home away from me. Do you remember how he tried to saddle me with the house I couldn't afford, then tried to tell me he'd allow me to pay him his half of the overinflated valuation in a year? There's no way I could have made that happen."

She frowned. "I still say if you'd been more forgiving, he'd have stayed with you. Sure, there were babies to consider, but as long as he was your husband . . ."

I began to worry about my parents' marriage. "Mom, does what you're saying come from personal experience?"

"That's none of your business," she snapped at me. "And don't you dare read my thoughts either."

Studies have shown that when you tell a person not to think about something, that's about all they can think about. It was the same for telling someone not to read their thoughts. Before I realized it, I saw a flash of my father with another woman, and he was holding a young boy in his arms. Did I have a brother somewhere on the island? "Fine. I won't," I lied.

"And another thing," she continued. "If you insist on staying on the island, the least you can do is come and visit us. And don't tell me your job keeps you too busy, because you know you can visit your father in the middle of the night."

Yeah, right. The middle of the night when I should be sleeping. "And I'd sleep when?" I snapped at her. "You act like the divorce is my fault, but it isn't. Quite frankly, I'm sick of it and I'm done having this conversation with you. I'm a grown woman and I don't need to defend my choices to you or anyone else."

I took a deep breath. I'd never spoken to my mother like that and, grown woman or not, I felt a little shaky.

Her eyes flashed with anger. "You ungrateful child. Is this what I get for trying to keep you safe?" She calmed her voice down and continued. "You don't know the lengths I tried to go for you."

"What do you mean?" I asked. She'd never said anything like this to me before.

She closed her eyes and took a deep breath. "I tried to move off the island when you were a baby, but your father wouldn't let me. I wanted to make sure you were normal. You had a good chance, better than most other people here, and I thought if I could get you away from here then maybe you'd be free to live a happy life, like everyone else in the country."

"But you couldn't go, because," I guessed, "Dad wouldn't let you?"

She nodded. "It's not always safe to have these abilities, and I thought if we could avoid the situation altogether you'd be safer."

I thought I knew a little bit about my powers not being safe. When they first appeared last year, I was sick and had a dangerous bout of vertigo that landed me in the hospital. It was only after I returned to the island that my symptoms went away.

"Some people can live off the island, even with their talents, but your father couldn't. He'd never be able to find a job that guaranteed he'd be out of sunlight for the entire year."

That made sense. I wasn't sure how well his skin condition excuse would work off the island. "I never knew. But mom, you have to give up on the idea of me leaving the island. It's too late now and I'm afraid that if I leave, I'll get sick again. Can we just call a truce? I don't want to argue anymore."

"Are you sure you won't leave the island? What about Kelsey? What if she wants to come visit?"

"I don't know. I'll try to keep her off the island by visiting her. It'll be a good test for how I feel when I'm not here. I'd rather not explain the island to her, not until she's older and can keep a secret." She'd never been able to keep a secret, and I wasn't sure if she'd ever develop the ability.

"Oh, there you are," Jack said as he turned the corner of the building.

He sounded a little too casual, and I suspected he'd been listening to our conversation.

"We need to get back to work, I've got a lead we need to run down," he said.

A lead? We'd barely started working on Randy's case. "Oh, okay." I turned to my mother. "I'll call you later this week, maybe we can meet for coffee."

She smiled. "I'd like that."

Jack and I walked toward his car. "Did I time that right?" he asked me.

I scowled at him. "I thought you were listening. But yes, you did. Much more and it was going to get awkward."

We climbed into the car and I asked, "What's the lead?"

He laughed. "No lead. I was just rescuing you. This is your case, so you need to go find your own leads."

Chapter 3

After the funeral, I looked into Marge's uncle. In this job, no one tells you the entire truth. It made sense to check into Randy first. If nothing came up with him, I'd move on to the four cottage residents. Jack was at his desk, reading the Gazette and taking notes.

Randy's life was not very exciting from the outside. He grew up on the island, married his high school sweetheart, Karen Williams, and lived a quiet life. Tragedy struck when Karen died four years after their wedding, and they had no children. Her obituary didn't list a cause of death, but I was sure my mother would know something.

I turned to Jack and cleared my throat to get his attention. "What do you know about Karen Petit's death?"

He set the paper on his desk. "Nothing. She died before I started PI work, and I haven't had reason to look into it. Have you got something?"

I stood. "Not yet. There was no cause of death listed in the paper, and I want to know more."

A small smile lifted the corners of his mouth. "Good. Frankie should know something."

She probably would, but I didn't want to go to her all the time. "I'm checking with my mother first. She and Karen were the same age and might have been friends."

Jack nodded. “Two conversations in one day? Things must be better between the two of you.”

Better, yes. Good, not yet. “I can make an effort, and it’s a lot easier if we have something to discuss.”

My mother was outside, weeding her herb garden. She looked up as I walked across the lawn. “Rebecca, what are you doing here? I thought we were going to have coffee later this week.” She stood and brushed the dirt off her hands.

After our conversation earlier, she sounded happier to see me. “I’m working. I’m looking into Karen Petit’s death. The two of you were in school together, and I wondered if you were friends.”

My mother sighed. "We were. Her death hit me hard, because she was the first friend I ever had that passed away."

Tears filled her eyes, and I felt a pang of regret bringing up sad memories for her. "Let's go inside and I'll make you a cup of tea."

As we walked across the lawn, a random thought occurred to me. My mother loved her gardens. She had an herb garden and a flower garden. She also spent a lot of time trimming the hedges and doing other yard work. What if her love of gardening was a way for her to get away from my father for a bit each day? I filed that thought away for another time.

I busied myself making tea while she washed her hands and sat at the table. "Were the two of you close?"

"We were. But my whole class was close. You know how it is growing up on the island."

Yeah, I knew. You were either friends with everyone or friends with no one. “It must have been tough for everyone when she died.”

She closed her eyes. “It was. Cancer doesn’t usually take someone so fast.”

I set two mugs of tea on the table and sat next to her. “Cancer?” I asked as I dropped my mental shields.

“Two weeks from her diagnosis to her death. She hadn’t even come to terms with it yet, hadn’t told anyone but Randy.”

My mother was telling the truth, or at least the truth as she knew it.

She took a sip of tea. “I just wish Randy hadn’t insisted on a closed coffin. I’d have liked to see her one more time.”

I put my hand over hers. “I’m so sorry, mom. That must have been difficult.”

“It was. But why are you asking about her? Who hired you to look into her death?”

"She's not the main focus of my investigation, but I was wondering about her. I can't tell you what I'm working on now, but it's not her. Did you ever think there was something suspicious about her death? Like maybe someone was lying about it?"

"Why on earth would anyone lie about that? She wasn't a healthy woman, and I suspect if she'd seen a doctor sooner she might have lived longer, but those last few weeks were brutal for her. I wouldn't have wished that on anyone."

She went to the living room and returned with a Shadow Island High School yearbook. She set it in front of me and pointed to the photo of Karen Williams. "This is how I like to remember her."

I looked at the smiling red-haired woman in the photo. She didn't look ill to me. "Was she sick in high school?"

My mother sat next to me. "No, she didn't get sick until after. She always made jokes about Randy being too much of a slob and making her work too hard around the house. Looking back, I wish I'd made her see a doctor. Twenty three is too young to die."

She was right there. I wondered if the police had investigated her death. I couldn't ask Connor, though, because he'd figure out who my client was right away. I didn't think I could ask anyone else for help, because they'd have to check with Connor first.

On the sidewalk in front of my office, I pressed the unlock button on my key fob. The chirp of the car made the family in the car next to mine look over at me. I waved and they waved back, not sure who I was. No one locked their cars on Shadow Island, but I hadn't adjusted my mind to the idea that the island was a safe place to live. Some people didn't lock their houses either, but after living in Boston with triple locks and a security system, I doubted I'd ever go that far. Especially not with someone breaking into houses.

I drove through town, to the dirt road that led to Randy's beach cottages. A memory flashed in my mind, making me shudder. I'd just driven past the spot where we'd captured Eddie Harrison and saved Corinne Baxter. If she hadn't been telepathically yelling as loudly as she did, I might never have heard her, and who knows what would have happened.

The beach came into view through the trees. A minute later, I pulled up to the first cottage and parked. I'd almost rented one of these, but the lack of bathtub was a deal breaker for me. My apartment had a lovely, deep tub. Some days it was a beautiful antique claw-foot beauty, and others it was a sleek, modern tub with whirlpool jets. I still hadn't decided which I liked better, but I supposed I didn't have to.

Lulu Sandoz lived in the first cottage. Her bike was propped up against the side of the house, so I decided to talk to her first. Each of the cottages were spray-painted in black with phrases like "give it back," "it's mine," and then devolving into swears and slurs. I shook my head. When Randy had described graffiti, I'd expected some tagging, not threats. And I wondered, what would someone be looking for in all four cottages?

After I knocked on her door, she opened it as wide as the chain lock would allow. "I'm not interested in whatever you're selling," she said. Her thoughts were a lot less polite.

"I'm not selling anything, Miss Sandoz. Your landlord has asked me to investigate the break-ins you and your neighbors have had. Can I ask you a few questions?"

She closed the door, unlatched the chain, and let me into her cottage, her cane tapping on the wood floor. "'Bout time he's taking our complaints seriously. Have a seat."

Like her neighbor Mamie, Lulu was quite old. I was amazed that these women were able to live on their own. Unlike Janet's cottage, which I'd toured last year, Lulu's was almost bare. She had a table and chair by the kitchen, a bed in the middle of the room, and a small loveseat by the front window. I sat at one end of the loveseat while she dragged the kitchen chair to sit in front of me. "My cottage was broken into, but nothing was stolen."

"Can you think of anything someone would want to take from you?" I asked.

Lulu shook her head. "Nah, I don't have much. But I don't want much either. Too much stuff gets in the way of life, you know?"

I nodded to cover the surprise I felt that she was lying to me. I could clearly see a ring in her thoughts, and it seemed to be a small engagement ring. Well, there was no surprise she didn't want to tell me about it, not when it looked like it was her only valuable possession.

And I knew how she felt about having too many things. I'd had a lot of stuff in the house in Boston, and most of it hadn't made the trip with me to the island. I didn't miss it either. George had always been the one who wanted the latest tools and gadgets, not me.

Then again, it was easy to say I didn't need much when my apartment provided for me. "How about your neighbors? Is it possible the thief wasn't sure which cottage to break into?"

"Couldn't say. It's not like we all get together to polish our treasures every weekend. I put new locks on the doors and got my shotgun out of storage." A shudder went through her. "I don't want to use it, but I will if I have to."

"Let's hope you'll never have to." I stood. "Do you mind if I look around outside?"

"Go ahead. I didn't see anything out there when I looked yesterday, but maybe you'll find something I missed."

I circled the building, focusing on the three feet between myself and the outer wall. Still no new footprints, no trash, no disturbed plants. I didn't even see evidence of Lulu going out her back door. Once I got back to the front door, I stretched my neck. Maybe levitation was one of the powers the thief had. I started around the cottage again, this time looking away from it.

As I turned the corner, I began to admire the beach roses—until I saw the sole of a sneaker poking out from under a branch. I froze in my tracks. I'd seen just one dead body in my life outside of a funeral home, and I wasn't sure what to do next. Maybe it wasn't a body, maybe it was just an abandoned shoe. Holding tight to that hope, I approached the bush.

My coffee threatened to come back up on me when I recognized the side of Randy's face—pale and lifeless. "Oh, no," I whispered. This was supposed to be an easy breaking and entering case, not another murder. What was I going to tell Marge? I reached for the phone in my back pocket. My hands were shaking so badly that I couldn't dial, so I resorted to voice command. "Call Connor."

I should have called the station instead of his personal number, but who thinks clearly when standing over a dead body?

"Hey, Becks," Connor answered. "What's up?"

I took a ragged breath. "I'm at the cottages on the beach, and I need you here."

"Okay. I'm on my way. Can you talk and are you safe?"

I could hear him speaking urgently to someone else, ordering cars to my location. "I found . . ." I didn't want to say it out loud. "I found someone, dead."

His voice took on a soothing tone. "Okay, Becks. Here's what I want you to do. Go to one of the cottages and put your back up against the wall. I'll be there in four minutes. Until then, we're just going to talk, okay?"

I backed away from the bushes and pressed my back against Lulu's back wall. "I'm at the back of Lulu's house."

"Good. Do you have a gun?"

I didn't. I didn't know how to use one, and I'd never allowed guns in the house when Kelsey was growing up. "No. Do I need one?"

His cruiser siren started and made it harder for me to hear him. "You shouldn't. But we'll talk more about that later. Do you know who you found?"

I closed my eyes to try to block out the memory of what I'd just seen. "Randy. I only saw half his face, so I don't know what happened to him, but I'm pretty sure he's . . ." What was it with me and not being able to say what happened?

"Is anyone there with you?" he asked, still keeping his voice calm and soothing.

"I was talking to Lulu. I don't know if anyone else is here. I can check."

"No," he commanded. "Don't move until I get there."

I could hear his siren and my knees began to tremble. I sank down to the ground and put one arm around my knees.

"I'm going to hang up now, because I'm almost there. Wait for me right where you are."

I slowly looked up and saw him rounding the corner of the building, two other officers behind him. He lifted me up and pulled me into his arms. "I'm here. Let's get you into the car."

He led me to his cruiser and opened the passenger door for me. "I'll be back once I've taken a look at the scene. Do you want me to call Jack for you? Or your parents?"

I shook my head. "No. Definitely not them. I'll call Jack. You get to work."

He squeezed my shoulder before he walked off.

"Call Jack," I commanded my phone. The call went to voice mail. "Hey, it's me. Our client is dead. Or at least I think he's dead. Connor's looking at him now. I'm not sure what to do next." I hung up wondering if maybe my work on the case stopped here.

CHAPTER 4

Weariness overtook me, so I closed my eyes. A knock on the window startled me, and I almost yelled. I rolled down the window. "What the heck is going on here?" Lulu asked. "You in some kind of trouble?"

I didn't have the energy to explain. "No. Not me. You should go talk to Connor."

She snorted. "He told me to wait over here until he could send someone to question me. Me! Like I'm some sort of criminal."

I sighed. It didn't seem like she was going to go away. I let my mental shield down just enough to read her thoughts. She was angry her day off was being ruined by whatever this was. "Randy's dead. I found him in the rosebushes behind your house."

Her shock was genuine. "That can't be. Who would want to kill him?"

That was the question, wasn't it? Who would want to break into cottages he owned, then kill him? "I guess that's what I'll have to figure out."

She eyed me suspiciously. "You didn't just kill him, did you?"

"What? Me? Don't you think you'd have heard something?" I looked down at my middle-aged body. "I'm not exactly stealth material these days."

"Just had to check. Getting so you can't even trust people on the island anymore."

Jack appeared in front of the cruiser, and this time I did jump. I'd never seen him do that before. It figures that he'd teleport in just after I said I wasn't very stealthy. What a show-off! He gave Lulu a dazzling smile. "Excuse me, I need to speak to Rebecca. If you wouldn't mind?"

Lulu blushed. "Of course not, Mr. Magus."

He turned to me. "Are you all right?"

I nodded. "Freaked out, but unharmed. Thanks for coming so quickly."

"You called Connor first? Next time, call me and then him. I'd have liked to get a look at the scene before they cart away all the evidence."

I hadn't even considered calling Jack until Connor mentioned him. "Sorry about that. I wasn't thinking and called the police out of instinct more than anything else."

Jack looked away and Lulu gave him a small wave.

"You really shouldn't put the whammy on women like that. Someday one of them is going to expect a lot more from you than a smile."

"The whammy? I was born a prince of fairy and you've boiled down everything I am to . . . I don't even understand what that word means."

I felt a small smile curve the corners of my mouth. "Of course you do. You do your"—I waved a hand in the air—"thing, and women do whatever you ask them to. You put the whammy on them."

"Yes, but whammy sounds so undignified."

I rolled my eyes. "Fine. What would you call it?"

"I don't call it anything. People do what I ask them all the time. It's just who I am."

I furrowed my brow. "Have you whammied me? Do I have this job because you wanted me to take it?" I opened the car door and got out. He was taller than me, but I looked up at him and gave him my meanest glare. "I swear,

Jack Magus, I'll walk away and never come back."

He laughed.

That was my answer. I spun on my heel and started to walk away. I didn't need this stupid job where I found dead bodies. The bank was hiring, and that had to be a safer job.

"Wait, Rebecca," Jack said.

I stopped, but not because he told me to. I couldn't feel anything like a compulsion forcing me to do what he wanted. And I definitely didn't have the urge to giggle and wave at him.

Slowly, I turned around. "That's all you got?"

He shook his head. "Just like you can't read my thoughts, I can't influence your actions. That was one of the reasons I hired you. Life is tedious when everyone does what you ask."

I snickered. "I bet. So what's the plan?"

"We stay here, find out as much as we can from Connor. He'll want to talk to you soon, so make sure you ask him questions too."

Connor walked around the corner of the cottage. "Ask me questions about what?"

My heart sank. I didn't want him to think I was manipulating him for information on my cases. I decided to tell the truth. "Randy was a client. He wanted to keep his case quiet, but I suppose that's not feasible anymore. I'll tell you anything you want to know, but"—I looked around at the small group of islanders who were gathering—"in private."

Emmy walked up to Connor. "Coroner's ready, boss."

He nodded and turned back to me. "We're just about done here. Give your keys to Emmy, and she'll drive your car to the station. You can ride with me."

I wanted to protest, but I had no business driving if I couldn't make my hands stop shaking. I handed Emmy my jingling keys. "Thanks."

It felt good to sit back down, and I closed my eyes as Connor drove back into town. He let me relax until we got back to the station. He parked but didn't get out. "You okay?"

I opened my eyes. "It's been terrible a day. I thought I was looking for some high school kids breaking in on a dare. I wasn't expecting my client to wind up murdered." I looked at him, maybe it wasn't murder after all. "How did he die?"

"Shotgun to the chest," Connor answered.

"Lulu owns a shotgun," I said.

Connor nodded. "Officer Breen is bringing her in for questioning. She claims she hadn't used the gun, but it'd been fired recently."

"She didn't do it," I blurted out.

Connor opened his door. "What makes you say that?"

I followed him as he walked into the station. "We were talking, and she didn't have any guilty thoughts."

He brought me into his office before he said anything else. "As much as I want to trust your instincts, I've got to follow procedure here."

We sat and didn't say anything for a minute. "I need to know about your investigation. You said he hired you to look into the cottages being broken into?"

I nodded. I wasn't sure how much I should tell him, how much Jack would want me to keep to ourselves, but a man was dead and the police had to get involved. "The four tenants each said someone had broken into their cottage. Nothing was stolen, and the only evidence they had was their back doors were open. I didn't see any footprints or evidence of the locks being tampered with. I was looking into Randy this morning, because he'd have a set of keys. It didn't make sense he'd hire me if he were the culprit, but if Marge forced him to, he might have thought he didn't have a choice."

"Why were you up there today?" he asked.

I took a deep breath and blew it out. "Graffiti on the cottages. I wanted to take a look at it, and at the scene. I wanted to tell the women there to be careful, because this looked like an escalation and I didn't want them to get hurt."

"Instead, you found Randy."

I looked down at my hands. "Yes. Maybe he found who I was looking for. The thing is, he should have been safe out there in broad daylight. Lulu would have heard something."

There was a tap at his door. Connor motioned for Bea, the office manager, to come in. She handed us each a mug of tea and left without saying a word.

"It's a possibility. Right now I don't even know when he died, or if that bush was the crime scene. There are too many unknowns for us to speculate right now."

I furrowed my brow. "Why aren't you out there? Shouldn't you be in charge of the investigation?"

He shook his head. "Breen can handle it. He's got the coroner out there, and he'll make sure Breen doesn't miss anything. I'm here with you, which is also important, because you found the body. Another body."

Did he think this was my plan for a boring afternoon? Head out of the office and look for trouble? "Yes, Connor, I did. And yes, he was another client. It's not as though I accept my clients based on how quickly they're likely to die. Whatever happened to Randy was a horrible thing, and I'd like to find out who killed him. And I'd like to find Marge and spend the day with her. She's going to need all the support she can get right now." I stood. "So if you don't mind, I'm going to find her. If you need me, call."

Connor stood as well. "Hey, Becks, it's okay. I was going to bring you with me when I made the official notification so you could stay with her."

I felt foolish, thinking he was getting ready to hold me for interrogation. "Okay. Yes, I'd like that. I'm sorry—it's just that I'm not used to finding bodies."

He ushered me out of his office and to the parking lot, where we took his cruiser to the Gazette office. Marge wasn't at her desk, but we could hear crying from the conference room. I suppose we should have known the news would have gotten to her before we did. When we opened the door, she looked to me, then Connor, and started crying harder.

I crouched in front of her and hugged her. "I'm so sorry, Marge."

She took two heaving breaths to stop crying before she looked to Connor. "Who did it?"

"I'm sorry, we don't know yet. But I'm putting every officer I have on the case, and I'll have answers for you as soon as possible. In the meantime, I think you should go with Rebecca to her apartment. The area around your cottage . . . well, you don't want to see it just yet."

I looked up at him and scowled. Sometimes the truth didn't help, and he could have cushioned the blow a little. "You don't want to be alone tonight anyway. We'll call Ellie, get a pizza and drink way too much wine."

Marge didn't look like she was paying attention to anything going on around her. I stood and took her hand in mine. "Come on, honey, let's go back to my place."

She followed me out of the conference room. "Let's get your bag and we'll take your car. We don't need the whole town staring at you right now."

She took her purse out of a drawer and handed it to me. "You drive."

Of course I would. There was no way she was ready to operate anything more dangerous than a spoon. We got into her car and I drove the few blocks to my apartment.

The apartment had drawn the curtains and dimmed the lights. Soft music was playing and there was a small tray of fruit on the coffee table. "Have a seat. Do you want something to drink?" I asked.

She shook her head and sank into an armchair. "No. I don't want anything."

I poured us each a glass of water and joined her in the living room. I took an angora afghan off the back of the couch and draped it over her legs.

"I should call to make arrangements," she said. "That's a thing people do, right?"

I took her hand in mine. "Yes, but maybe we can wait for a day or two. We'll need to"—I struggled to find a way to put this gently—"wrap up the case first."

"Oh, right. You probably know more about that than I do." She closed her eyes and seemed to fall asleep.

I whispered her name after a minute, but she didn't answer. I pulled out my phone and texted Ellie to bring pizza and wine in about an hour.

I didn't want to leave her alone, so I started to write out notes on my laptop about the case. The problem was, I had very little to go on. I had no idea who had been breaking into the cottages, who spray-painted graffiti, who killed Randy, and if any of these events were linked.

Jack had taught me to write out everything I could, then worry about connecting the dots, so I got started.

After a while, there was a knock at my door. Marge didn't stir when got up and opened the door. Ellie was there with food, and Connor was behind her with two bottles of wine.

"Come on in," I whispered. "She's asleep right now."

I kissed Connor quickly. "Any updates?"

He shook his head. "Not yet. I thought I'd give her a quick report in person before I got back to work."

Ellie set the pizza on the dining room table, and we hugged. "I can't believe it. He was such a nice guy," she said.

She was right, he'd always been a nice guy, at least to us. But there must have been someone out there who thought differently.

CHAPTER 5

"Remember the time we wanted to build a water slide in your yard, and how your mother came running out of the house as we dragged the ladder through the flower bed?" Ellie asked.

Like I could ever forget that! Life on an island could be incredibly boring when school was out. We were old enough to be bored with the same games we played every summer, but too young to get jobs. Marge, Ellie, and I thought we could rig up a water slide with a ladder, a tarp, and a hose. We could charge fifty cents per ride, and we'd be rich by the end of the summer. At least rich for twelve-year-olds.

We picked my yard because it was the prettiest, and we all knew my dad slept all day so he wouldn't come out and yell at us. But when my mother saw us dragging the ladder through the lilies, she was out of the house and yelling like we'd never seen before. Marge and Ellie ran, leaving me to take the brunt of her anger. I didn't blame them, she was scary that day.

Uncle Randy got the story out of Marge that night, and he helped us set up a one-day-only water slide on his lawn. Free of charge to all the kids on the island. So much for our dreams of riches, but it was one of the best days I'd had.

And now that I was thinking about it, I was supposed to be grounded for the rest of the summer, but somehow my mother never followed up on that, and I didn't spend a single day scrubbing floors. I wondered if Uncle Randy had anything to do with that.

"How about the time we snuck out of the house and Uncle Randy saved our asses by lying to your mother?" I asked Ellie.

We both grinned as we remembered that night, where he lied so brazenly that Ellie's mother had no choice but to accept what he said and usher us home. We didn't get in trouble for that either. Was he like our fairy godmother? Who was he that our parents did whatever he told them to?

I wished I could ask my parents about this, but I wasn't certain they'd tell me the truth.

"I don't even want to tell you how many times he drove me home and talked to my parents for me," Connor said.

"Is that pizza?" Marge asked from the living room. She stood and tossed the blanket on the chair.

"We've got wine, too, if you want some," Connor said.

Marge's face paled. "Are you here with news?"

"Not yet. I wanted to check in on you and make sure you were okay," he said.

"I'll be a lot better once you find who—" she choked up and couldn't finish her sentence.

Connor put a hand on her shoulder. "I'm heading out to do that right now. You three behave yourselves, and I want to see at least one of those bottles empty come morning."

I grinned at him, facing away from Marge. "Yes sir!"

Ellie started dishing out slices of Mamma Gianni's pizza onto the plates I'd brought to the table. She had gone old-school and ordered plain cheese. A lot of cheese pizzas were plain and boring, but not Mamma's. The cheese blend meshed perfectly with the spices in her sauce to leave you feeling like you'd just tasted a bit of Italian perfection.

I opened the first bottle of wine, a bottle of chianti, and poured for all of us. "To Uncle Randy, protector of us all."

Ellie and Marge raised their glasses and we sipped quietly.

"While you were asleep, we were remembering some of the times Uncle Randy saved us from getting into serious trouble with our parents," I said.

Marge closed her eyes. "He was my protector, and because you were my friends, he protected you too."

"What I don't get is how he managed to talk our parents out of punishing us. I was sure I was going to be in huge trouble that day we decided to run away and live on the beach," Ellie said.

I smiled at the memory. We had it all planned out. We'd live on fish and learn how to start a fire with two sticks, because none of us had the foresight to bring matches with us. We only made it to just past dark before we were starving and cold that summer night. Uncle Randy came walking up the beach with burgers and frappes for us. We devoured them, and when he asked if we'd rather stay or go home, we all decided to go home because the sand fleas were starting to bite.

It seemed like such a reasonable choice to go home at the time. How had he talked me into it? "Marge, what was his power?"

Of course when we were kids we didn't know about powers or how people used them. Was he persuasive enough to get us home that night and to keep our parents from punishing us?

"He could make people do what he wanted, because he could show them the future," she answered.

I didn't understand. "He can see the future? Like he's a psychic?"

She shook her head. “Not exactly. He could only see the future if he was showing it to someone else. And he could show different futures based on actions people were about to take.”

My eyes widened. He must have shown my parents the futures I’d have with and without being grounded. “So that’s how he saved me from being punished?”

“I had no idea,” Ellie said. “I thought he just talked my parents into cutting me a break because I wasn’t a bad kid.”

“What would my future have been like if he didn’t talk to my parents?” I asked.

Marge shrugged. “He didn’t ever talk about it. He just went on with his day and never said anything to me, not even when I was old enough to know.”

“Then why didn’t he protect himself from whoever shot him?” Ellie asked.

Marge closed her eyes. "He didn't like his power and didn't use it for himself. He said it was best if he used it to give people a nudge in the right direction, not plot out their best future. He didn't like the way knowing the future could strip away a person's free will."

That seemed reasonable. I couldn't imagine consulting with someone over every possible decision I could make. There would be no end to the amount of time I could take from him, and then multiply that by all the people on the island? That would be too much for any person to handle. It was amazing he used his talents for us so often.

"And he never used it for his own life?" Ellie asked.

A tear slid down Marge's cheek. "I guess not. I wouldn't want to see when I'd die, or when I might die." She stood. "I think I'd like to be alone for a while, if you don't mind."

We got up and hugged her. "Of course not. You can have my room, and I want you to wake me up any time you want. If you want to talk, or scream, or just sit quietly with someone else, I'm here," I said.

"And I've got tomorrow off, so I'll be here in the morning," Ellie said.

Marge shuffled off to my room and closed the door.

Ellie started to clean up our dinner. "I'm going to head out, unless you need anything else."

I shook my head. "No, I'm fine. I'll do a little work and have an early night myself. Tomorrow I'll start working on the case."

She looked confused. "What case? You're still going to find out who was breaking into the cottages?"

"Yes. And I hope that'll lead me to who killed Randy. Connor won't like it, but Randy paid us a retainer, and we at least have to work on the case until it's spent." And there was no way I would stop until I had all the answers Marge needed.

We hugged and she left.

I let out a big sigh of sadness for my friend. She had no other family on the island and was all alone. Once my parents and I stopped talking to each other, I thought I was alone, but that wasn't true. Kelsey was still there for me, and in an emergency, so were my parents. In a true emergency, I might even be able to go to George's parents. Not that I would, but they might be better than nothing.

A new door next to my bedroom caught my eye as I straightened up the apartment. I opened it and found I suddenly had a second bedroom. "Thanks," I whispered as I walked in and changed into my pajamas that were laid out on the bed for me.

I made myself a cup of cocoa and settled down with my laptop to do some research. First

I looked through the registry of deeds for everyone who had owned the land the cottages were on. In the past three hundred years, the land had been owned by Randy, his parents, his grandparents, and before them a man named Lenox Stewart. I wasn't familiar with the surname, and was pretty sure there weren't any of his family still on the island.

Next I went to the town's vital records and searched births, deaths, and marriages of this Lenox Stewart and his relations. He passed the land to his daughter, and it stayed in her family until they sold it to Randy's grandparents.

I wondered what happened that they decided to sell beachfront property. Even on an island with no tourism, it was still valuable. But that was a question for the newspaper archives and maybe some of the older people in town.

I shut down my laptop and finished getting ready for bed. It was going to be a difficult week, and I needed to make sure I was at my best for Marge and the investigation.

Chapter 6

The next morning I decided it was time to talk to Frankie. She must have heard something by now.

I opened the door to the diner and stepped in. To my horror, George and Chloe were ordering breakfast. "What are you doing here?" I asked.

He turned and smiled at me. "It's a small island, and I was sure I'd run into you here. We need to talk."

To his side stood Chloe, trying to quiet the twins in their stroller. She looked to me and I could tell something was wrong. She was upset and looked like she hadn't recovered from seasickness. As much as I didn't want to read the minds of my friends, George and Chloe were fair game.

Jack stood behind me. He hadn't been there a moment ago. "You okay here?"

"No. They need to get off my island."

George flashed his best financial management smile, and I wondered how I'd never realized how fake that smile was. "We have some financial details to iron out first."

"Let's get them across the street so you can talk in private," Jack suggested.

I didn't want George to know where I worked, but there was no way I was going to feed the town gossip mill any more than I needed to by talking to him there. "Good idea, Jack. George, let's talk in private."

George and Chloe followed me, kids still fussing in the stroller. I took the time to read George's thoughts. He was angry. Angry with me because he had to pay me alimony, angry with his boss for canceling his mid-year bonus, and angry with Chloe for not keeping the twins quiet. I remembered how frustrated he would get when Kelsey didn't settle down for him. Chloe was in for a difficult few years with him.

Chloe, on the other hand, was worried. She didn't think he'd be able to talk me into lowering my alimony and then she'd be stuck with him and his temper on the long trip back to Boston.

Once we crossed the street, Jack suggested we go to my apartment. My large, beautiful apartment would only anger George more. "Are you sure about that?"

"Absolutely," Jack said.

There was no elevator in the building, so George and Jack carried the heavy double stroller up the stairs. Chloe and I followed behind them. "Sounds like the boys aren't having a good day."

She bit her lip. "There's never a day when they don't cry. I think I'm a bad mother."

And just like that, my anger with her turned to pity. "Babies cry. It's just a fact of life. You go through the steps to make sure they're comfortable and then you just hold them, talk to them, read to them, whatever it takes until they settle down."

Her eyes widened. "But that's so much work. I have other things I need to do in my day."

And the anger was back. "You squeeze what you can into the times when they're napping and let everything else go. They'll only be babies for a short time, but in this short time, they're learning whether or not they can trust you."

She said nothing, but her thoughts weren't kind. It was fine if she didn't want to believe me. I was right, but it took a very confident woman to take parenting advice from her husband's ex. Hopefully someone else would tell her the same thing and she'd listen.

My apartment door was scuffed and dirty, and as I unlocked it, the number fell off. "Sorry about that, I haven't had time to do much maintenance yet." I pushed the door open and looked inside. My apartment had changed itself from its usual large, airy, gorgeous floorplan to a one-room studio with dirty laundry on the couch.

I was mortified. The apartment and I were going to have words later on. I didn't know if it heard me when I spoke to it, but it would at least feel my embarrassment later. I rushed in and began picking up the laundry. "Sorry about that. I wasn't expecting guests." I looked around for a laundry basket, but couldn't find one. In desperation, I opened the only door I could find and tossed the laundry into the bathroom. The bathroom was much larger than I expected, and it had several other doors. I stepped in, closed the door I just walked through, and opened the next door on my right. I saw Marge sleeping in her bedroom. I didn't have time to check the rest of the doors, and I just assumed the rest of the apartment was behind them.

"Please, have a seat," I said.

George and Chloe sat on the couch, while I sat on the unmade twin bed across the room. Jack sat at the tiny kitchen table that had at least three meals' worth of dirty dishes stacked up on it. I appreciated the apartment not making me look like I was spending a lot of money on it, but I'd never been this much of a slob.

I brought my focus back to George and Chloe. "What are you doing on my island?"

George flashed what he thought was an endearing smile at me. In the past, that smile would have gotten him whatever he wanted, but I knew better now. Even without reading his mind, I knew there was no way I'd give him anything he wanted. "You didn't answer any of my voice mails, and I was worried about you."

He looked around and continued. "But obviously I don't need to. Look at you, Becks, doing so great on your own. You've got this apartment and a job and really, everything you could need."

I rolled my eyes. "Great. Now that you've checked up on me, you can go. As you said, I've got a job and I need to get back to it."

George looked to Chloe. She shook her head and he glared at her. She wrapped her arms around herself. "George is right. You're a completely independent woman now. And because of that, we were hoping you'd be willing to voluntarily reduce your alimony payments. For the children."

She said for the children, but her thoughts said she wanted a nanny because she didn't want to be a mother. George's thoughts, however, weren't centered on a nanny. He wanted an occasional babysitter and a nicer car.

Before I could say anything, Jack cleared his throat. "Speaking as Ms. Wright's attorney, we're not going to do that. As I recall, your income should be sufficient to provide for your ex-wife, your current wife, and your two new dependents. Has anything changed?"

George looked down at his hands, then back up at me. "You remember Stanton?"

"George's vice president. Very involved in the business. Likes to keep an eye on upper management," I explained to Jack.

"He's also a moralistic jerk. He didn't like how quickly I married Chloe and decided I hadn't earned the quarterly bonuses I'd always got. I was counting on that money for the boys."

Chloe reached over and took George's hand. In the most rehearsed tone I'd ever heard, she said, "I just don't know if we'll be able to give the boys what they need if we don't find more money."

I looked at Chloe's expensive shoes and purse. "You could sell a few things on PoshMark. Maybe go back to work."

Chloe pulled her purse closer to herself. "This was a gift from my parents. I can't sell it."

George stood up. "You know my wives don't work. You didn't work, why would you want Chloe to? She has twins and trust me, they're more than double the work. She needs help with the boys."

What a jerk! I'd just seen he wanted to spend most of the money on a new car. Unfortunately, I couldn't tell him that. "It doesn't matter to me one way or the other whether Chloe works. You've got to deal with the consequences of your actions. Maybe you could get a second job? Buy a cheaper car? Sell your new house? I'm sure there are ways you can economize. Maybe Chloe's parents can give you a loan."

"We're done here," Jack said. "Enjoy your drive back to Boston."

Jack took the stroller and pushed it out the door, forcing George and Chloe to go with him.

I walked down to the office and watched the three of them put the babies and the stroller into George's new Land Rover. He'd probably have to sell that soon. Those poor kids.

After they drove off, I went back to the diner. When I walked in, Frankie put her tray down and gave me a big hug. "You were married to that jerk? No wonder you came back home."

I laughed. "If only it hadn't taken me so long to figure it all out. Can I get a coffee to go? New case, and it's been a busy morning already."

She walked behind the counter and poured me a cup. "I was about to call Connor when you and Jack got here. You should let him know your ex was in town. That's not the kind of thing a man likes to hear through the grapevine."

I took the cup from her once she put a lid on it. "It's not important. They'll go back to Boston and it'll all be over."

I turned around to find Connor standing behind me. "What'll be all over?"

My day just kept getting better. "Can I talk to you outside?" I asked.

He held the door open for me. "It's not a big deal," I said. "George was in town with his wife and the twins."

Connor raised an eyebrow. "Oh yeah? What did they want?"

I rolled my eyes. "He wants to pay me less alimony. Chloe, his wife, wants a nanny and he's not making as much as he used to."

"You said no, right?"

I laughed. "I didn't even get the chance. Jack said no for me. Because he was my divorce attorney, not because he's my boss. Anyway, don't worry about it. They'll have a terrible drive home where they'll yell and argue, the babies will keep crying, and they won't bother me again."

Connor adjusted his gun belt. "You sure? What kind of car was he driving? I'll keep an eye out for him."

I put my hand on his arm. "Honestly, that's not necessary."

He gave me his best, sternest cop face.

"Fine. He's driving a silver Land Rover with Massachusetts plates. But I tell you, he's going to take the next ferry."

He took my hand in his. "Promise you'll call the station if you see him, okay?"

"I will, but they're not going to hang around here. They're probably already off the island," I said.

He kissed me on the forehead, because that was what passed for romance while we were working. "I'll call you tonight. If nothing exciting happens, you can finally make me that dinner you've been promising me."

I'd been teasing him with my recipe for garlic and rosemary lamb for weeks now, saying I was saving it for a special occasion. I went back to my apartment, just to make sure it was back to normal. I unlocked the door and the dingy, small room that George thought I lived in was gone.

"Thanks. But maybe next time you don't need to throw my dirty laundry around, okay?"

The apartment never answered me, but a small vase of flowers appeared on the kitchen counter. "I accept your apology."

I opened the fridge to grab a snack and saw a package wrapped in brown paper and tied with twine on the top shelf. Lamb Chops was written on the top. "Thank you," I said as I grabbed a serving-sized bag of grapes. I was going to become very spoiled living here.

CHAPTER 7

I went down to my car, hoping I was right and George would leave on the next ferry. I needed to put him and his laughable financial troubles out of my mind and get back to work.

The first thing I needed to do was go back to the cottages. I didn't need to inspect the crime scene, although I probably would. I needed to focus on my own case—who broke into the cottages, and who painted the horrible graffiti on them. The cases had to be linked, but by sticking to what Randy had asked me to investigate, I'd be out of Connor's way and perhaps I'd find the killer before Connor did.

Not that it was a contest.

Okay, it was totally a contest. George hated it when I turned things we did into a contest, because he didn't always win. When he did win, I made sure it was hard work. After a year or two he started to get nasty, and I shut down my competitive nature to preserve my marriage. I smiled, excited to have the spirit of competition urging me on.

I drove the now familiar road to the cottages and parked in front of Lulu's cottage. I was relieved to see no signs of crime scene tape or other police presence. Each cottage looked dark and empty, and I mentally kicked myself for not checking to see if the occupants were home. They probably weren't, because who would want to sleep next to a murder scene?

I got out and knocked on Lulu's door anyway. Even if no one was home, I could take a look around the outside of the buildings for clues I'd missed yesterday.

To my surprise, Lulu opened her door a crack. "Go away. You're not police, and you don't have a warrant."

"Please, I just want to talk for a few minutes. I'm not police, but you know Randy hired me to find out who was breaking into the cottages. I don't want to quit the job just because he's gone. It would be an insult to his memory, don't you think?"

I hoped my off-the-cuff argument would convince her. I expected she'd want to help with the investigation.

Lulu slammed her door shut, and I was about to walk away when I heard her slide the chain off the latch. "Fine. I'll talk to you, but I've only got a couple minutes before I've got to get back to work," she said as she swung the door open to let me in.

I smiled at her. "Thanks. I won't take much of your time."

She'd slid her bed from the middle of the cottage to the wall, just by the bathroom door. The loveseat she'd had by the window was now where the bed was, along with a new area rug.

"You've moved your furniture around," I commented.

She sat on the loveseat, propped her cane on the arm rest, and motioned for me to join her. "Didn't feel right, being exposed like that. Now when I sit and look out at the ocean, it takes more work to look in at me."

As she spoke, I could see the ring she was hiding and smiled. The ring was under a loose floorboard, under the new rug. I wasn't sure a new furniture grouping would prevent its theft, but if the burglar hadn't found it yet, it wasn't what he was looking for.

She'd also bought shades for the large window. They were open now, but once the sun went down I was sure she'd close them. "If you don't feel safe here, I'm sure you could find a place to stay for a few days in town. I don't think it will take the chief long to find Randy's killer."

It felt a little odd calling my boyfriend the chief, but it was also too informal to refer to him as Connor.

Lulu scoffed. "That boy? I remember when he couldn't tell the difference between left and right, and didn't have the sense the good lord gave a turnip."

I snorted with surprise. "Really?"

"Oh yes, I used to watch him and Ian when his parents wanted a night out. Lovely boys, but not blessed in the brain department. I caught them trying to jump off the roof because they were convinced the blanket they were holding would work like a parachute."

I laughed, imagining the two of them holding the edges of a blanket, working their nerve up to jump off the roof of their house. "It's a good thing you were there. I think he's grown into a much smarter man than you give him credit for. He's a little young to be the chief, and that's got to count for something."

"I suppose so. But he's not good enough to have kept Randy alive."

"That's not fair, though. Connor didn't know what was going on up here. If Randy had gone to him straightaway, things might have turned out differently."

As we were talking, I wondered why she felt her ring had to be hidden. The diamond was small and overall it couldn't be worth more than about five hundred dollars. I tried to search her thoughts, but all I could see were her thoughts of our conversation about Randy.

"Maybe, but Randy was stubborn and didn't want police all over his business. It had to be important to him if he was willing to give us a break on the rent."

Landlords weren't known for charging less rent, so she was right. "Do you know why he wanted to keep Connor away?"

She frowned. "No. I assumed he had something here, maybe in Marge's cottage, that he didn't want anyone to know about."

I hadn't considered that. I paid close attention to her thoughts as I asked my next question. "Like what?"

Her thoughts were of no help. "Beats me. He's a good man, not inclined to mischief, so I don't think it's anything to worry about. Maybe Marge will find whatever it is once she gets settled in."

I wondered if Marge would be settling in, or if she'd go back to Pete. "You think she's going to stay here?"

Lulu laughed. "I have no doubts. If you'd seen her when she first drove up with a car stuffed full of her things, you'd think so too. A woman doesn't take all her possessions if she's only planning to be gone for a week."

I tried a new tactic to get Lulu to think about the ring she was hiding. "I wonder if she'll give Pete back the wedding and engagement ring?"

Lulu's mind flashed to her ring, then to a young man I didn't recognize. He was in his early twenties, and his vintage military hairstyle screamed fifties. This must have been her fiancé. Her next thought flashed to a coffin with a flag draped across it. Had he died in battle? Viet Nam? No, that was later. Korea.

"She'd better not. Those rings are gifts for her to keep, no matter what happens. Even if they never married, for whatever reason, she keeps the engagement ring."

Her mind flashed to arguments with a couple that I assumed were her fiancé's parents. They demanded the ring back and she refused. Surely they had passed away by now, and there wasn't any reason to keep the ring hidden. Unless his siblings still wanted it. This was a question for another time. Could they be the ones breaking in, looking for the ring?

I wasn't sure. Wouldn't they only go into Lulu's cottage and not the other three? It was another clue to look into. But I couldn't imagine someone shooting Randy over a ring he didn't even have.

"I don't want to keep you any longer. Thank you for talking with me. And if you think of anything, no matter how small, that might help with the case, please call me."

Lulu grasped her cane and used it to stand up. "I will. You're not so bad, young lady. A lot better to talk to than the chief. You can come back anytime."

When I quickly checked Janet's and Mamie's cottages, no one was home at either one. I'd have to come back out here later this evening.

I decided to go home and check on Marge over lunch. She was still sleeping when I left, and I didn't want her to spend too much time alone. I opened the door to see her sitting on the couch, staring out the window. "Hey, Marge. How are you this morning?" I asked quietly.

She didn't answer.

I sat next to her and put my arm around her shoulders. After a minute, she sighed. "I'm okay. I'm still trying to get used to the idea though. Randy's gone, I'm probably getting a divorce, and I'm afraid to go back to my cottage. Nothing in my life is the way it should be."

"I know, and it sucks you're going through all this at once. If it helps, you can stay here for as long as you like. I've got plenty of space, and if you go through with the divorce, I can sympathize with you. Also, did you know Jack's a lawyer? I'm not sure you can hire him for your divorce, but I bet he'd be willing to talk to you about it."

I stood and walked to the kitchen. "I'm only here for lunch. Do you want me to make you anything?"

"The apartment has been trying to get me to eat all morning. Every once in a while, a plate of food appears by my mug, but I don't have any appetite. I've barely had any of my coffee."

I pulled a can of soup from the cabinet. "Has it made you tomato soup and a grilled cheese sandwich?"

She stood and brought her mug to the kitchen sink. "Not yet. If you make it for me, I'll at least take a few bites."

I kissed her on the forehead. "It's a deal."

Marge sat at the dining table and fidgeted. "Can I ask you about your divorce?"

I buttered a slice of bread. "Of course. Ask me anything you want."

"How did you know your marriage was too far gone to be saved? When did you decide to leave George?"

I sighed. I didn't know and was blindsided when he decided to leave me. "I didn't. George did the leaving, not me. I would have stayed with him, probably forever, if he hadn't decided to leave me for Chloe."

"Oh. I thought you left. Why would he leave you? You're amazing."

I grinned at her. "Thanks. I was getting sick and we didn't know why. He didn't want to take care of me and decided he'd rather trade me in for a younger model. An older, sick wife isn't as impressive as he feels he needs to be."

She looked surprised. "And this woman he left you for?"

I rolled my eyes. "It's so cliché. He left me for his assistant. Apparently they'd been seeing each other since I first started getting sick, and by the time I was in the hospital she was pregnant and he didn't see any reason to stay with me. Not when he could have a family."

"That creep."

I nodded. "It gets worse. He and his new family were here today, asking for me to voluntarily give up some of my alimony payment."

Marge had been looking at the paper, but her head whipped up when she heard this. "He came with his new wife and kids?"

I put the ungrilled sandwiches on my griddle and poured the soup into a pan to heat. "He has no idea what could happen, bringing babies onto the island. What if they grow up and have powers but don't know where they came from? They certainly won't have anyone to guide them. When he called yesterday, I thought it would only be him. Who wants to drive for four hours with two babies, then take a ferry?"

"Maybe he thought you'd be swayed by the twins?" she asked.

They were very cute, but all I felt for them was pity for having the parents they did. "It didn't work. And I doubt they'll be back. Chloe was dealing with serious seasickness."

"Good. We don't need them here."

I flipped our sandwiches over and stirred the soup. "So what are you planning to do about Pete?"

She ran her hands through her hair and sighed. "I think I have to leave him. It can't be good for any of us, especially the kids, for us to be fighting all the time like this."

They'd fought from the moment they started dating, and I never understood why she stayed with him.

"If we were fighting about important things, that would be one thing. But we fight about the stupidest shit—did I fold his socks the wrong way, or did he put the trash barrel in the garage wrong," she said.

I plated our lunch and brought it to the table. "George and I fought like that for a while, then we just stopped talking to each other for the most part. That probably should have been a warning to me, but I was so grateful for the peace in the house that I didn't realize how bad our marriage had got. Looking back, I should have left him sooner and taken Kelsey out of that environment."

"Thanks. I think I should get the kids out of the house. We can't all fit in the cottage, but I can find us an apartment on the island. They deserve to live in a home where they aren't worried about people fighting all the time."

"You can ease into it, you know. Divorce is a big step, so you can start with a trial separation, and you can both decide what you want to do next. One thing I regret is not having gone to couples therapy. I think we could have worked out a lot of our issues and maybe not split up." I took a bite of my sandwich. "But that might be wishful thinking. I'm not sure George has enough respect for me or my feelings to make therapy work."

Marge put her spoon down. "I hadn't considered that. I'm sure I'll see Pete around town, and I can suggest therapy to him. I don't think he wants to break up the family, but we've fallen into a rut of bad communication and can't seem to get out of it."

I hoped that was true and my friend could finally have a happy marriage. "Do you mind if we change the subject? I'd like to ask some questions about the cottages."

Marge looked worried. "The cottages? Are you still investigating the break-ins? I don't think I can pay you for that."

"Don't worry about that. It's the least I can do after all Randy has done for me over the years. And do you mind if I ask some questions about him too?"

She nodded slowly. "I think I can talk about him without crying. What I don't understand is why he allowed himself to get shot. He was a seer—he could see the future, Becks. He knew what was going to happen."

"I don't know. Maybe he couldn't see what would happen to himself very well? Maybe the future where he didn't get shot was so bad he felt he had to sacrifice himself? Maybe he was protecting the people who lived in the cottages?"

Marge didn't last long not crying. She brushed a tear away. "The bitch of it is, I don't think there's another seer on the island to ask."

There ought to be a list of who had what powers, I thought. What good was it to have the ability to help other islanders but to hide it away because of some idea that we didn't talk about our powers? "Can't we ask around?"

Her eyes widened. "People over fifty don't talk about their gifts. It's like they all walk around, pretending they're normal all the time. Only in the past five years have some of the younger people embraced their new gifts and allowed other people to see them. There's a lot of backlash with their parents' generation, though, and so for the most part, no one knows who has what power—or, if they do know, they definitely don't let on."

I frowned. That was ridiculous. In a town where people with special talents were the overwhelming majority, there was no reason to be afraid. "I think we should do something about that. But for now, can you think of anything Randy might have said or done to indicate he was afraid for his life?"

Marge closed her eyes and thought. "No. But if he knew something bad was going to happen, he wouldn't have told anyone. Especially if he was trying to protect someone else."

This made me even sadder. How long had he been going through the motions of normal life, knowing he'd be shot and killed yesterday?

"Do you think, I mean, if it was inevitable that he would be murdered, that the killer was at fault? I mean, what if he couldn't avoid his fate any more than Randy could?"

"Hmmm," I said. "I'm not sure any of our actions are inevitable. I like to think we've got free will. If Randy had decided not to go to the cottages yesterday morning, he might still be alive. Yes, something worse might have happened, but we'll never know what that might be. I think his killer could have also made different choices, especially since he probably wasn't a seer. He'd just be going along in his life making choices that could have led him away from Randy altogether."

"You're probably right. And I want him found and tried. I was just thinking about this this before I got out of bed, and I wasn't sure how to reconcile the idea that he might not have had a choice over his actions. But like you said, Randy chose to go to the cottages, even though he knew what would happen. That same free will must be available to the rest of us."

CHAPTER 8

Even though my apartment made an excellent cup of coffee, some days I preferred to grab some from the diner. Frankie was a great source of information about what was going on in town and if she wasn't busy she'd tell me almost anything I wanted to know.

I sat down and she poured me a cup. "Hey, Frankie, what do you know about Karen Petit's death?"

She put the coffee pot down. "Karen Petit, there's a name I haven't heard in a long time. Why do you ask?"

"It's just background for the case Randy hired me to work on. I can't find a cause of death listed anywhere. My mother said it was cancer, but if that were the case, why wasn't it listed?"

Frankie sighed. "I forget you don't know everything about the island. Sometimes a person doesn't take well to their ability. They're not strong enough to handle it and it eats away at them. We call it the cancer because we don't want to be reminded that it can be dangerous to live here."

I took a sip of my coffee. My parents forcing me off the island made a little more sense now.

"But don't you worry about that. You're doing just fine. I heard you and Connor were kissing in the Filet parking lot last week."

I blushed like I was fifteen and caught doing something I shouldn't have. Just because my face felt like it was on fire didn't mean I could let her have the last word. I was a grown woman and there was no shame kissing anywhere I wanted to. "We were. And wow . . . I swear it felt like I'd never left the island or him."

She waggled her eyebrows at me. "That good? You better hold onto that, honey. You know what it's like when the spark goes out of a relationship."

Didn't I, though? George and I had stopped kissing, talking, or even watching television in the same room years before I realized there was a problem. "I'm doing my best. What's the gossip around town today?"

Frankie surveyed the two tables of customers before she started in on the day's news. "Other than you two kissing, there's the sad news about Randy, and something about vandalism out at the cottages."

I nodded and took a sip of my coffee. "The cottages were spray-painted with some really awful words. I don't know who would have done that. Do you have any ideas?"

Frankie put a blueberry muffin on a plate and slid it in front of me. "Eat. You need strength to keep up with that boyfriend of yours."

Great. I was blushing again. All we'd done was kiss last night, but Frankie seemed to think a lot more was going on between us. "The vandalism?"

"Oh, right. Every once in a while, a few high school kids get hold of some spray paint and decide to tag a building. It's usually the school or town hall though. I don't think I've ever heard of someone's house getting painted."

"How about Randy? Do you know anyone who was angry with him?"

Frankie laughed. "Angry with Randy? He was the nicest guy around. I can't think of anyone who would want to hurt him. No, for my money I think he stumbled on something he shouldn't have seen, someone panicked and shot him. No one would have planned to kill him."

That had been my thought as well, but I'd been off the island for so long I didn't know how things may have changed.

"Troy Torres was angry with him, and they almost came to blows in the Hannaford parking lot, but I can't see Troy shooting someone over a land deal," Frankie said.

Troy owned the town's only construction company. In a town where most houses were passed from generation to generation, he was always looking for new projects. "Aren't the cottages a little small for him to worry about?"

"He wanted to pull them down, clear the trees behind them and build an oceanside resort. He wants tourism on the island, no matter what the cost."

I couldn't imagine the town's zoning board allowing him to build anything to attract tourists. Strangers weren't particularly welcome on the island, for their own good. "And Randy didn't want to sell?"

She put her hand on her hip. "Of course not! No one will sell to Troy. No one wants to be responsible for what might happen to the tourists, even though the money they'd bring to the island would be nice."

Frankie looked over my shoulder, made a quick sour face, then smiled. "Afternoon, Mrs. Wright. What can I get for you?"

My heart sank. I'd never hear the end of it if she saw George before he left the island. "Hi, Mom. Do you want to sit here with me?"

She took the stool next to me. "Tea and a slice of pecan pie, Frankie."

Frankie went off to assemble the order, leaving me with my suspiciously happy-looking mother. "What's up?"

"You didn't tell me George was in town."

Crap! I thought I'd got him off the island quickly enough that no one would have noticed. "How'd you hear about that?"

Frankie set tea and pie in front of my mother and turned to fold napkins. Within an hour this entire conversation would be all over the island. "I didn't hear about anything. He stopped by the house with coffee and donuts."

My worst nightmares were coming true. Even though we were divorced, I'd never get rid of him. "Was he alone?"

She added milk and sugar to her tea. "Of course he was. You don't bring someone with you when you visit your wife's parents."

I took a bite of my muffin. "Ex-wife."

"That's the thing, though. He said he'd made a horrible mistake and that he'd take you back in an instant. All you have to do is say the word."

Frankie stifled a laugh and walked off with a pot of coffee.

"Say what word? Say I'd take his lying, cheating, cheap ass back?"

My mother scowled. "Rebecca, mind your language."

It was too much to believe. "No, I will not. He's lucky cheap ass is the worst thing I called him. Let me fill you in on the rest of the story. He and his wife—his new wife—came to see me earlier today. They wanted me to voluntarily decrease the alimony I receive because he needed more money for the twins. So if he's still here, he's here with his new family."

My mother looked confused. "I don't understand. Why would he take his new family to ask you to come back to him?"

She was so dense sometimes. "He wouldn't. He was lying to you. Manipulating you to come talk to me. He doesn't want me, he just wants more money."

"But he seemed so sincere."

"Yeah, well, he's not." And as if on cue, I heard babies crying outside the diner. I turned to look out the window and saw George, Chloe, and the babies about to come in. He recognized me and instantly hustled his family out of sight. "See? George, Chloe, and the twins are here on the island."

My mother's face went white. "He brought the babies?"

I could not take it anymore. "Of course he did. He's got no idea it might not be safe for them here, because I had no idea." I pulled a five-dollar bill out of my wallet and threw it on the counter. "You know what? I'm done here. I can't take any more of this—not from him, and not from you."

I stormed out of the diner and followed George into the town convenience store. I could hear Chloe complaining. "But honey, you promised me a real sit-down meal."

He turned on her and scowled. "Do you want to eat in the same restaurant as her? I know I don't."

"You can eat at the diner," I said as I approached them. "Your wife deserves a hot meal at the very least."

By the time George faced me, he had a grin on his face that didn't show in his eyes. "Rebecca. Good to see you again."

"I thought I told you to get off the island," I said.

He chuckled. "You did, but it's such a beautiful vacation spot we couldn't help but take a day to see the sights. In fact, we're thinking about staying for a week. Maybe two if it suits us. Besides, Chloe's stomach isn't ready for the ferry."

I rolled my eyes. He'd be itching to leave by the third day he was here. "You've already missed the last ferry of the day. If you're not gone by noon tomorrow, I'm calling Stanton to let him know you're harassing me."

"You wouldn't," he said.

I pulled out my phone and started scrolling through my contacts. "Let's see, I'm pretty sure I've got his number here somewhere. Oh, there it is." I held the phone up so he could see I wasn't lying. "Maybe I should just call now? Save everybody time and aggravation. I'm sure your boss would be happy to hear from me."

His hand darted forward to grab my phone, but before he could touch it, Connor was between George and me. If you didn't know anything about his shifter abilities, you'd think he appeared out of thin air. But no, he could just move very fast if he wanted to.

"What seems to be the problem here?" he asked George.

George looked Connor up and down and decided he didn't want any trouble with the local police. "Nothing, officer. Just a misunderstanding between my ex-wife and myself."

Connor gave George a look that made him shrink back behind the stroller. Coward. "That's Chief. And you're having a misunderstanding with my girlfriend."

George's face went red. "Really?" He looked around Connor to me. "You've been on the island for how long, and you're already dating?"

What was it about this day and people saying the stupidest things? I didn't answer, I just looked to Chloe and then the babies.

"If I see you on the island tomorrow, I'll arrest you for disturbing the peace. Is that clear?" Connor asked.

George nodded. "I guess you can get away with that sort of thing up here in the sticks."

Connor let that comment go. "I want you on the first ferry out tomorrow morning. I'll have an officer watching to make sure you leave."

George turned and started walking toward his car, Chloe and babies following in his wake.

"The boat leaves before the crack of dawn, you could have at least given them time to eat breakfast," I said.

"They can eat on the mainland. I thought you said they were gone."

I sighed. "I thought they were. He went to talk to my mother alone this afternoon, telling her he'd take me back."

He laughed. "How'd that go?"

I turned to face my office. "Walk me to work and I'll tell you."

We walked down Main Street and I told him what my mother told me. "She was completely willing to believe him, right up until she saw him with Chloe and the boys. Are you really sending someone to watch the ferry for him?" I asked.

"Do I need to?"

I thought for a minute. "Yes. In the moment, George will do what you tell him, but the further away he gets from you, the less likely he's willing to follow your orders. By the time he gets back to the hotel to pack up, he'll be questioning whether you have the authority to tell him never to come back."

Connor smiled wryly.

"Do you have the authority to keep him off the island?"

"Technically, no. Not unless it was a matter of safety. I can order people on or off the island in case of emergency."

It was going to be an emergency if I saw him again. "We don't have to tell him that, though."

Connor used his shoulder mic to call into the station. "Send whoever isn't busy to the hotel in a marked cruiser. They're looking for a—" he looked to me.

"Silver Land Rover."

"—Silver Land Rover with Massachusetts plates. Watch them for the rest of the night and follow them to the ferry in the morning. Assist them in making the six o'clock boat if necessary."

The dispatcher confirmed his orders.

"That's right. And don't be too discreet. If they give you any problems, call me back and I'll take care of it personally."

I raised my eyebrow at him.

"Can't order my people to intimidate someone. That's got to come from the top."

I stopped at my office door. "Thanks for your help. With any luck we won't see him again."

He opened the door for me. "Let me know if he bothers you before he leaves."

I didn't like the tone of his voice. "You're not going to do something . . . wolf-y . . . are you?"

Connor laughed. "No. I'd get in touch with the police in his town, let them know what's happening here and ask them to keep an eye on him for me."

I gave him a quick kiss on the cheek. "You're my knight in a shining badge. Talk to you later?"

He nodded and walked toward the station.

Chapter 9

I spent the next hour looking into Troy Torres before I went to interview him. On paper, he was a wildly successful businessman, especially for being limited to working on the island. He was one of the people I saw in my mother's thoughts when I first learned the secret of the island. Troy was a selkie and needed to spend time in the water, in his seal form, every day. He couldn't cover up that sort of transformation working on the mainland. He was in his late fifties and had never married.

Every time I'd seen him around town, he always seemed busy, a little stressed out, and about to yell at whoever was with him. Everyone else on the island had a much more laid-back attitude on life. He didn't fit in on the island, but he was stuck here. I never thought to be grateful that my ability would allow me to leave the island whenever I wanted. As long as the nausea and vertigo didn't come back, I could spend as much time on the mainland as I wanted to. I had more freedom than many of the island residents.

The secretary at Island Construction was very friendly on the phone and gave me the location of Troy's current build site. He was building a house on the rocky cliffs on the west side of the island. I drove out to the location and was surprised by the size of the foundation. The house looked like it would be about five thousand square feet. Not large for the suburbs of Boston, but practically a palace compared to the modest capes and one-story ranches here on the island.

I flagged down the closest construction worker and asked for Troy.

"Rebecca? Is that you?"

I looked more closely at the man carrying a box of nails. "Yann? Is that you?"

Yann and I had gone to school together. I suppose that wasn't a surprise when you grew up on an island, though, was it? He'd been the varsity soccer captain and led the school to the state championships two years in a row.

He put his box down and opened his arms wide. "I heard you were back on the island. It's good to see you again."

We hugged and then stepped back. "Do you need to talk to the boss today? He's not in the best of moods right now."

"Yeah, I do. If you just point me in the right direction I'll find him myself."

Yann shook his head. "No can do. We've got rules for site visitors. Follow me."

He led me to the portable office. It had four desks, a small table and a countertop with a coffee maker and boxes of snacks. “You’ve got to sign in here and wear a hardhat at all times.”

I signed my name and purpose of visit on the log and took the blue hard hat from him. “I’ll take you to the boss, then escort you back to your car. Blue hats aren’t allowed on site without an escort.”

“The blue hat means what, exactly?” I asked.

“It means you’re a visitor, and it’s like a warning to keep an eye on you, because you don’t know what’s dangerous here.”

I was fairly sure I knew what was dangerous on a construction site—basically everything. Having Yann keeping me safe was a good thing though. “Lead on.”

We walked across the site where at least a half a dozen men I recognized were working. “Who’s the house for?” I yelled as we passed Joe

Duncan, another high school friend, who was cutting plywood with a circular saw.

Yann rolled his eyes. “Don’t ask.”

I didn’t ask, but I got a clear picture from his thoughts. Troy was building the house to impress a woman he met online so she would move to the island. What was it with him and bringing more people here? There weren’t any laws about people moving to the island, or off it either. Residents were free to move off the island, provided they kept its secrets. The town as a whole didn’t want strangers moving onto the island, and the only reason there weren’t any laws keeping people off is that no one wanted to have that sort of thing written down.

Torres was looking at blueprints spread out on the tail of a black pickup truck.

“Hey, Boss!” Yann yelled over the noise of the construction site. “Got a visitor for you.”

Torres turned and looked disappointed to see me. I guess I wasn’t the woman he was hoping would show up. I took a deep breath and held out my hand. “Nice to meet you. I’m Rebecca Wright with Magus Investigations. I’d like to ask you a few questions.”

He didn’t take my hand, but nodded for me to follow him. We walked until the noise of the site faded enough that we wouldn’t have to yell to hear each other. Yann stayed by the truck.

“What does Jack Magus want with me?” Torres asked.

“Well, ah,” I stammered, intimidated by the dismissiveness in his voice. “I’d like to ask you about Randy Petit and the land you wanted to buy from him.”

“That guy? Isn’t he dead? Don’t tell me his family wants to sell the land now, because I’m not interested.”

I couldn’t believe how callous he sounded. “Yes, Mr. Petit was murdered. I’m investigating the vandalism and home invasions that occurred at the cottages in question.” Okay, so home invasion might be stretching what happened a little bit, but I felt like I needed to sound more important to keep his attention.

"Don't know anything about that. I wanted to buy the land and tear down the cottages. It's a great location for a resort I've got planned. He didn't want to sell, so I moved on. End of story."

"I heard you two had argued over the sale. Did the argument ever get out of hand?" I asked.

He stared down at me. I wasn't short, but he was a foot taller than me and used every inch to try to intimidate me. "No. Listen, I don't know you, but I know your boss. I've already answered these questions from the police, and I don't have the time or the patience to answer them again from some wannabe rent-a-cop. So why don't you go back into town, write up your little report and make sure to say that Troy Torres doesn't kill to get his way."

By the time he was done speaking, he was yelling at me. I straightened to my full height and stared into his eyes. "You don't? But you need to intimidate women by yelling at them, and honestly, it's a slippery slope from intimidation to actual crime. Why don't you start by telling me why you weren't at Herbert Krawczyk's funeral yesterday?"

"No."

That was all he said. It didn't give me much to work with, but there was no way he would win this fight. "Fine. I'll check the uncooperative witness box and start a thorough investigation into your finances and your bizarre need to bring outsiders onto the island. Because of you, we may finally get the rules for island residence codified into law."

"You wouldn't. But I've met someone and she wants to see my house," he said.

I looked behind me at the construction site. "This house? The one you haven't even built yet?" I turned back and said in a condescending tone, "Did you lie on your dating profile? That's another area Magus Investigations can clear up for you. We can send her photos of your house as it is today. I doubt she wants to come to a loud, dirty, construction site. Don't you?"

He looked over at the site. "It will be done in a month."

I didn't know much about how long it took to build a house, but when my friend Zara built a house in Newton, it took twice as long as her contractor's estimate and cost almost three times as much. I suspect the cost overruns were Zara's fault, though. If she hadn't insisted in upgrading almost everything she said she wanted in the house, she might have come in closer to budget. Still, if Troy hired enough people, I supposed the house could be finished in a month.

"Okay, so she comes in a month. Then what? How are you going to explain your ability to her?" I knew I was off topic, but I wanted to get him as off-kilter as I could before I asked him about Randy.

He grimaced. "You don't know if I've got anything. Besides, it's undignified to talk about it. I don't understand why the younger generation insists on telling their every secret to anyone who will listen. Look at that ridiculous book Prince Harry put out. Trust me, no one wants to know everything about a person."

I rolled my eyes. "Trust me, the seal has been broken on your secret." Now that he knew I knew his ability, I asked the one question I wanted to know the answer to. "What happened the last time you saw Randy Petit?"

His mind instantly flashed to the parking lot of the grocery store. Troy was yelling at Randy and standing so close to him that he was pressed up against his car. The last thing Troy said before he stomped away was, "Fine. I'll come up with another way to get what I want."

This could be interpreted as a threat, or not, depending on what his next steps were. If Torres started making offers on other beachfront property, he was probably in the clear. And given that this was the last time he'd seen Randy, he didn't kill him.

"Get out of here," he practically growled at me.

Yann rushed up and took my arm. "Time to go, Rebecca."

His grip was firm and he pulled me away from Troy. "Stop, you're hurting me," I told him, more because I didn't like being pulled around like a naughty kid.

Yann let go of my arm. "Sorry. I tried not to grab you too hard. You don't want to get the boss mad though. Trust me."

"How bad is his temper? I mean, would he get someone to hurt me?" Or maybe that was what he did to Randy.

"What? No! You spent too much time in the city if that's what you think."

We walked back to the field office so I could sign out and return my hard hat. "You know what he wants to do on the island, right? How can you work for him when he wants to bring in tourists?"

Yann sighed. "Look, Becks, it's a job and I've got a family to feed. Those kind of decisions need to be made by the mayor and the town council, not me. If I quit, he'd hire someone else and the only thing that would happen is that I'd miss my mortgage payment. If you want him stopped, you'll have to get the mayor on your side first."

We left the office and started walking to my car. My black Lexus stood out among the old, battered pickups the construction workers drove. "I'm sorry. You're probably right. I just can't imagine how our lives would change if the secret got out. All it would take was a few people coming for vacation, having their kids developing a talent once they grew up, and then tracing it back here. I'm imagining teams of government scientists coming to study the island, and residents being tested. I don't want that for us."

He opened my car door for me. "I don't either. But like I said, there's nothing I can do."

I drove off, thinking about what I could do. I had assumed no one wanted to bring more people to the island, but was that true? If Yann was one or two paychecks away from not being able to pay his mortgage, then a lot of other people here might be too.

Once I finished this case, I'd make a point to go talk to him.

I decided to snoop around at the police station before going back to the office. Maybe I'd pick up a few clues and if I was lucky, I'd set up a date with Connor too.

Bea greeted me as I walked in. "Good to see you, Rebecca."

"Thanks, Bea. You too. Is he in?"

"He's been going over reports for the last hour. I'm sure he'd like a distraction by now."

I smiled. "I can do that." I stepped closer to her desk. "Between you and me, have there been any breaks in Randy's case?"

She shook her head. "None that I know of, but they're all working on it. Just about everyone in town respected him, and I can't imagine who would do this. I almost want to say it had to be someone from off the island, but who would come all the way out here to kill a stranger?"

I shrugged. Had George been on the island when Randy was murdered? What was I thinking? He wasn't even man enough to confront me about a divorce. He tried to move out while I was in the hospital. There was no way he'd shoot a man.

I knocked on Connor's door. It took him a moment to yell for me to come in. As I opened the door, he was hurriedly stacking folders on his desk. He beamed when he saw me. "Becks. You are the ray of sunshine I need right now."

I sat in a visitor's chair. "Bea told me you were going through paperwork. Want to grab dinner? A man cannot live by paperwork alone, you know."

He put the folders in a drawer and locked his desk. "Absolutely. I don't remember having lunch. Where do you want to go?"

I thought. "Not Filet. As much as I love Ian's cooking, I feel guilty not paying for any of it. How about the clam shack?"

His eyes lit up. "I could go for some fried clams and onion rings. Let's get out of here."

The shack was on the small boardwalk by the docks. As we parked near the ferry to the mainland I looked for George's car. "Did George leave this morning?" I asked.

"He did. Breen had to wake them up and monitor their packing. His wife complained the whole time that he said this would be a vacation and so far all they'd done was hang around the hotel and eat in a diner."

I grinned wryly. "Good to know I'm not the only one he lies to, I guess. Did I tell you he lost his regular bonuses because his boss is upset that we're divorced?"

As we walked into the clam shack, Connor looked confused. "Serves him right. I'd never do something to drive you away."

I stopped walking and stared at my gorgeous date. I was so lucky to have found my way back to the island. "It's all about money with him. His boss really liked me and when he found out George left me, work started getting more difficult. George wasn't getting the bonuses he used to and it turns out he needs that money to stay afloat. My guess is that he can't pay his bills without it. He'd rather leave Chloe and go back to me, just so he can have all the things he wants."

We sat at a table and took the menus propped up between the salt and pepper shakers. "That's not a healthy motivation, not when it causes you to ruin the lives of other people."

I put my menu back. Who was I kidding? I already knew what I wanted, the fisherman's platter with extra tartar sauce. "I agree but, then again, George has never been much overly concerned about other people."

He put his menu back and held out his hand across the table. I took it and grinned at him. "How's Marge feeling today?" he asked.

"I had lunch with her, and she's doing about as good as you can expect. I want to ask questions about the break-ins, but I don't have the heart to yet."

"You're not still pursuing that case, are you?"

It was time for the inevitable my boyfriend is worried about my job and I need to take better care to stay safe lecture. "It was the last thing he ever asked me to do. Of course I am. I'm focusing on the weird lack of theft and trying to figure out who's been going through the cottages. I'm not looking into his death."

Connor cocked an eyebrow at me.

"Okay, okay, I asked Troy Torres if he killed Randy, but only because he was trying to intimidate me, and he deserved to have me read his thoughts about Randy."

"And?" he asked.

"He didn't do it. The argument they had in the Hannaford parking lot was the last time Troy spoke to him."

"Inadmissible, but I'll move him to the bottom of the list for now."

Bonnie Chevalier, Ellie's niece, came to take our order. "Hey, Aunt Becky. Good to see you two here."

I smiled at her bright cheerfulness, even though I hated being called Becky. In the short time I'd been back on the island, the kids in Marge's and Ellie's families had started calling me their aunt as a term of endearment and respect for the longstanding friendship I had with their mothers. "Hi, honey. I'd like a fisherman's platter with extra tartar sauce and a lemonade."

"You got it. And for you, Chief?"

"Fried clams and onion rings. And another lemonade."

"Coming right up." She leaned over a bit and said in a mock whisper, "Tell me, when am I going to start calling you Uncle Chief?"

I blushed furiously, he blushed, and Bonnie laughed at the two of us. "No pressure, but it's obvious you're crazy about each other. You're old enough to think marriage is important so why wait?"

She left and I sank down in my chair, hoping the other patrons didn't hear her. "I'm mortified."

He looked everywhere but at me. "The innocence of youth. It's not as easy as get back together and get married."

He was right. I wasn't even close to ready for anything resembling a commitment yet. George had hurt me deeply, and it wouldn't be fair to Connor if I rushed into marriage before I was ready. "No kidding. I wish I had her outlook."

Bonnie came back with our lemonades and thankfully said nothing as she set them on the table.

"It's not that I wouldn't, you know, but we've both got a lot of baggage and things to work through before we can talk about major commitments."

I nodded, knowing I had a whole lot of issues to work through, but I didn't know what he meant for himself. Had he dated a woman, or several women, who hurt him badly? I wasn't going to ask over dinner—that's what friends were for. I'd ask Marge and Ellie.

"Are you having any luck with the murder case?" I asked to change the subject.

"We're narrowing our suspect list. We've got a few potential motives but honestly, we're grasping at straws right now."

"You don't really think Lulu killed him, do you? She was at the funeral, I saw her there."

Bonnie dropped our food off. "Looks ominous over here. I hope you didn't take me seriously before."

"Like we'd take relationship advice from someone as young as you," I joked.

She smiled and walked away.

Connor took a bite of onion ring. "No, I don't think Lulu killed Randy. She hadn't shot the gun recently, and it was a mistake to bring her in."

"Got anything else you can tell me? My side of the case isn't looking any clearer than yours."

"I don't. And dammit, Becks, you know the rules. No talking about work."

I squinted at him as I took a sip of my lemonade. "That's not entirely accurate. You don't tell me anything about your work but you expect me to tell you all about my cases. But let's just change the subject. What are your Thanksgiving plans?"

"I'm sure Ian will cook something amazing for the four of us. My mother loves his cooking almost as much as she loves not having to make large family dinners anymore. You know he'd love to have you there, right?"

I did. In fact, I was sure that if I didn't at least go over for dessert, Ian would take it as a personal insult. "I haven't heard anything from my mother yet, but I can't imagine they're doing much." Thanksgiving was never a big deal at my house, not with my father grumbling about how he had precious little to be thankful for.

"Great, I'll tell Ian you'll be there. We eat at noon, which should give you time enough to at least visit your parents too."

CHAPTER 10

Connor dropped me off at my apartment right after dinner because I brought Marge a cheeseburger and strawberry frappe. She hadn't been eating much, and I hoped the comfort food would tempt her appetite.

Unfortunately, she was asleep when I got home. It was only eight o'clock, but I didn't blame her. There was only so much time a person could devote to grief in a day before it got to be too much.

The frappe went in the freezer and the burger went in the fridge. I looked around and realized I didn't want to do anything else with my night either, so I got into pajamas and climbed into bed with a new book.

I fell asleep with the light on and woke to Kelsey's ringtone on my phone. "Hey, honey, is everything okay?" It was seven in the morning, which made it four in California.

"Yeah, I'm fine. I wanted to call you before you got busy for the day. I miss you and really want to come home over Christmas break. Everything is weirdly warm here, and I really don't want to go to Dad's again this year."

I smiled. Weirdly warm sounded good to me. "Oh, I don't know, Kels. I don't have a lot of space in my apartment for you. How about if I come spend break with you instead? I could use some warmer weather about now."

"Dad told me about your apartment, and I thought I could maybe help spruce it up a little."

I groaned. "He caught me at a bad time. I promise it's not as bad as he thinks. A fresh coat of paint, a hamper for my laundry and a few rugs and it'll be just fine. That's hardly worth you flying all the way from UC Berkeley for."

"Are you sure about that?" she asked.

"Definitely. I promise. Why don't I look into a plane ticket and hotel for the week of Christmas and get back to you."

I didn't like lying to her, but I couldn't explain how her father had been deceived by a sentient apartment that only showed him what was best for me. I'd have to find a way to send her photos of an apartment that looked like my dingy one, but was spruced up and looked better so she wouldn't worry. Maybe I could ask the apartment to dress itself down a little bit for photos.

"He wasn't sure what you were doing for work, but that your lawyer was there when he and Chloe were visiting. What's that about?"

I felt like we'd strayed into dangerous territory. I didn't want to lie to her more than necessary, but her father could get information from her that I didn't want him to have. "It's a small town and people look out for each other. Did your father tell you that my lawyer made it possible for him to marry Chloe so quickly?"

"Uh, no, he didn't. He said you'd hired some underhanded crook who would use any trick in the book to get what you wanted."

I sighed. "Well, I'm sure he said that. The bottom line is that through my attorney's ability to facilitate compromise, both your father and I got most of what we wanted. But you don't want to hear about all of this, and I don't want to rehash it this early in the morning. Are you up for the day or are you going back to sleep?"

She yawned. "I'm getting up in a few minutes. Liz and I are going out for a run before breakfast and then we're going to study until our first class."

That sounded horrible to me. While I had to produce a lot of work as a fine arts major, I never had to wake up early to study for the kinds of exams a physics major had. "Test today?"

Kelsey laughed. "No. Chemistry test next week. There's a lot to learn and we're not sure he's going to let us use a periodic table. We don't study for tests the day of—too much stress."

She was right to study ahead of time, but I doubted she'd make it much further into her college career before she started cramming for exams. "So who's Liz?"

"She's another pre-med physics major and she lives down the hall. We're thinking about being roommates next semester. Her roomie is an art major, and the room always smells like paint and chemicals. And I'm not happy with my roommate either. I mean, she's fine, but she's out until two or three every morning and wakes me up when she comes in. At least with Liz we'll be on the same schedule."

"Sounds fair. Do you have to apply to switch?"

"I don't know. I'm going to talk to my RA today and find out. So, can I tell Dad you're coming here for winter break? He wanted me to come spend break with him, and I don't really want to."

That made me sad. "Why not? I hope you're not letting what happened between him and me damage your relationship with him. Marriages don't always work out, and it's not always someone's fault. People just grow apart and decide they'd be happier with someone else, or even alone." I mentally applauded myself for taking the high road.

I heard her blankets rustling as she got out of bed. "Yeah, that might be true for some people, but the honorable thing to do is to end one relationship before you start another one. You don't knock up your assistant and then decide you want to divorce your wife."

True, that was the right way to do it, but hardly ever how it played out.

"And he left you when you were sick. If he weren't my father, there's no way I'd even give him the time of day. And neither would you, now that you're not married to him."

"I know, but I just don't want to see you throwing your relationship with your father away on my account. You should decide how you want to relate to him based on how he treats you. If you find he doesn't treat you well, I'll back you up with anything you want. But don't base your relationship with him off of mine."

I could practically feel her eyes rolling through my phone. "Fine. But I doubt we're going to make it for very long. I got the distinct impression he wanted me to watch the twins while he and Chloe went out. He was looking more for a babysitter and less for a daughter."

"You won't have to worry about that, because I'll be with you in the warm sun. I could use a little vacation."

She sighed. "Can you afford a ticket and a hotel? From what Dad said, you've basically got nothing. I could chip in, and you can stay in my dorm with me."

I laughed. "There's no need for that. Your father was exaggerating. I have a good job and the ticket won't be a problem."

We hung up shortly after that and I lay in bed, thinking about how close to sounding like my parents I'd gotten. I was ready, in that call, to do everything I could to keep Kelsey off the island and keep her from developing strange powers she wasn't ready for.

But was that the best thing for her? Some people moved off the island after they got their powers, but I had no idea how life was for them. Did they hide their abilities? I couldn't imagine they showed them off. Were they treated any differently if they confided in friends? I'd have to look into that.

I knew most people stayed on the island, or maybe moved to the mainland but stayed close by. And of course it made sense that some people had to stay on the island. Connor could live anywhere, because he could control his shifting. I wasn't sure how I'd do off the island. Maybe my illness would come back, and maybe it wouldn't.

The question was, did I want to take that chance with Kelsey? If I thought she'd have a useful and yet invisible gift, absolutely. But what if she didn't? I'd be condemning her to life on the island whether she wanted it or not. She'd never finish med school and her plans for the future would be crushed.

No, it was best to keep her off the island. She was amazing enough that she didn't need additional powers to get along in life. All I had to do was make sure she didn't feel like I didn't want to see her. Visiting her regularly was a small price to pay for her to stay the way she was.

I was beginning to feel some sympathy for my parents, or at least my father. It was no wonder he didn't come to visit me—how could he hide the fact that he couldn't go outside during daylight? I would have come up with something to do that might have harmed him, and at that point he'd have to either pick a fight and go home under cover of darkness, or tell me the truth. I doubted he would have wanted to do either.

And I guess my mother wouldn't go because my father wouldn't. It had been a big deal for her to show up at my hospital room after I fell. Had she told my father he was on his own and had to do without her or had he told her to go and not worry about him?

I could go round and round all day wondering what made my parents tick, but I had a case to work on, and with any luck, a murder to solve.

Chapter 11

I threw the blankets off my legs and got out of bed. If my daughter could be up this early, so could I. I wasn't surprised to see Marge up already, sitting on the couch. "Hey, sweetie, how are you feeling this morning?"

She looked up from the paper she was reading. "Better. I got a lot of sleep last night, and I feel like I can start making arrangements for Randy."

I walked into the kitchen and poured myself a mug of coffee. "Want some?"

She shook her head. "I'm sticking with herbal tea right now. The apartment thinks it's best for me." She got off the couch and grabbed a slice of toast from the toaster. "Do you mind if I have someone over this morning?"

"Of course not. You can do whatever you like while you're here."

She smiled. "Good. Because he'll be here in a few minutes."

I looked down at my pajamas. Plaid flannel shorts and a tank top, not exactly what I wanted to greet guests in. "Thanks for the warning. I'll get dressed and then get out of your way."

"You don't have to leave. Adam Krawczyk is coming over to help me figure out what I want to do for the funeral. I thought I should get advice before I go to the funeral home."

"Okay, I'll be right out." I closed my bedroom door and chose my outfit for the day. Jeans, baby blue cashmere sweater and sneakers. It wasn't late enough in the year that I needed to worry about snow, so boots weren't necessary yet.

When I opened the door, Marge was leading Adam into the living room. "Nice place here. I guess working at the paper pays the big bucks," he said.

Marge laughed. "It's Rebecca's place, not mine. I live out at the cottages, where Randy was found."

"Oh. I'm sorry," he said.

There was an awkward silence between them that I broke by offering Adam coffee. He declined, but at least we weren't all standing around looking at each other. "Why don't we sit at the table so Marge can take notes," I said.

Once we sat and I slid a notepad and pen to Marge, she started to explain her situation. "I want to do right by Randy, but I can't spend a lot of money. I might be in the middle of a divorce and I can't ask my husband for money right now. If you don't mind, can you tell me how much you spent on everything and if you thought it was worth it or not."

"Yeah, sure. The casket was the most expensive part of . . ."

I stopped paying attention and started thinking about my case. Why would someone kill a seer? To keep secret something he saw. To cover up a crime that hadn't happened yet. Great, how could I solve a crime no one had committed? Short of reading the thoughts of everyone on the island and hoping they were thinking about this supposed future crime, I had to find more clues.

". . . and that's all I spent," Adam wrapped up.

Marge had taken a page of notes while I wasn't paying attention. "Thanks so much, Adam. And I'm sorry I didn't say it before, but I'm sorry for your loss. Your uncle was a fixture here on the island, and it just won't be the same without him."

I bit my lip so I didn't snort with laughter. Herbert was definitely a fixture in town, sort of like an old rusty tap that never really shut off.

"Hey, Marge, I just thought of something," I said.

They both looked at me. "Did your uncle ever write down the things he saw? Maybe he left notes about what was going to happen to him?"

She furrowed her brow. "I don't know. No one was allowed in his study, no matter what. I always thought it was because we were kids and would mess up his papers, but even as adults he would lock the door before leaving the room to come talk with us."

"Interesting. Do you feel up to looking around his study this morning?"

She stood quickly. "Absolutely. The sooner we figure out who killed him, the safer we'll all be."

"I'll just see myself out," Adam said. "It sounds like you have a busy day of investigating."

We rushed out of the apartment, on our way to Randy's house, excited by our new line of investigation.

When we got to the first floor of the building, Abby stepped out of the office. "I was just coming to find you," she said.

"We're kind of in a rush, Abby. What can I do for you?" I asked.

She opened the door wider. "This will only take a minute. If I could speak to you privately?"

I looked to Marge. "Do you mind? I'll be quick."

Marge shook her head. "I'll wait here. Do what you need to."

"Mr. Magus has been called off the island. He wants you to update the regular clients this week."

I rolled my eyes. We had a few regular clients who were certain they were being watched, followed, or somehow spied on. They weren't. I asked Jack why we continued to work for them when we'd proven they were wrong. He said it gave them peace to know we were watching out for them and they were willing to pay for that peace.

I thought they needed a different kind of professional help, but kept that thought to myself. "Okay. I'll take care of that as soon as I get this case put to bed. Was there anything else he wanted me to do?"

She shook her head.

"Okay. Marge and I are going to Randy's house. Call me if you need anything else."

Marge and I rushed to Randy's house, eager to investigate his study. I turned the handle to his front door, but it was locked. "Tell me you've got a key. I don't want to explain to Connor why we broke in."

"Of course I do." She took her keys out of her purse and unlocked the door. Neither of us stepped forward for a moment.

"Are you ready? I can go in alone if you want me to."

She sighed. "No. I'll have to go in sooner or later. No one else will clean out the house. I might as well get it over now."

I followed Marge into the house and wrinkled my nose at the smell of rotting food. Why would he have left food out if he knew what was going to happen to him?

"Oh, gross," Marge said. "I tell you what, I'll take care of whatever that smell is, and you start in the study. It's the second door on the left."

The study was unlocked and I let myself in. I closed the door behind me because it smelled much better in there. The room had built-in bookshelves loaded with books, newspapers, and magazines. There was one piece of paper on the desk, and I sat to read it.

<indent and italics> Dear Rebecca,

Thank you for taking care of Marge. She's trying to be strong, but needs all the support she can get.

I know you're here to find out who killed me. Lucas Bolen shot me by the cottages on Old Beach Path.

Tell Connor and let him arrest Bolen.

You have a long and happy life ahead of you,

Randy.

</indent and italics>

I took a photo of the note and left the room. Had Connor already followed up on this lead and not told me? We'd have heard if Bolen had been arrested. "Hey, Marge, I've got what we need."

She poked her head out of the kitchen. "Who?"

"The note said it was Lucas Bolen. Does that seem right to you?"

"Yes. He and Uncle Randy fought on and off for years. When they weren't fighting, they were the best of friends. I never understood how he put up with it."

Probably the same way she put up with arguing with her husband for so many years, but I didn't point that out. "We need to call Connor in now. We've got proof, and the note tells me to let him handle the arrest."

"You call. I'm going to look for a photo of him for the service."

After Marge went upstairs, I called Connor. "I know who killed Randy. He left me a note on his desk," I said in one breath.

"Hang on there. Slow down. Who left you a note where?"

I took a deep breath, regretted smelling the kitchen so deeply, and continued. "Randy left me a note on his desk. He said Lucas Bolen killed him."

"You're in the house now?" he asked.

"Yes. Marge is upstairs looking for a nice photo for the funeral."

"Shit. I want the both of you out of the house immediately. Stand in the driveway and wait for me to get there."

I didn't understand, but his tone left no room for argument. "Come quick." I hung up and yelled for Marge. "We need to go. Connor's worried."

She rushed down the stairs. "Connor's worried? About us being in the house?"

I nodded and pulled her toward the front door. "Something about the note. He said to wait outside until he got here."

She closed but did not lock the door, and we waited by my car.

Connor and Emmy arrived a few minutes later. "Do you have the note?" he asked me.

I held out my phone. "No. I took a photo of it, thinking you'd want it for evidence. Why didn't you take it when you searched the house?"

"Emmy, check the house," he commanded.

She walked through the front door, gun drawn.

I was starting to get a very bad feeling about this. "Connor, what's going on? This is about more than a missed piece of evidence, isn't it?"

He nodded. "There was no note on the desk when we searched the house. Let me see it again."

I handed him my phone, and he turned it to Marge. "Is this your uncle's handwriting?"

She enlarged the photo and stared at it. "I don't know. Maybe? I can't remember."

He put an arm around her shoulder. "That's okay. We'll find a writing sample in the house to compare it with."

"How did the note get there?" she asked.

"It's there to throw you off the trail of the real killer. Exactly what I didn't want, Becks. You promised me you were only looking into the break-ins," he said.

I put my hand on his arm. "I was. I had this idea that maybe he kept notes of his visions and maybe we could find what he saw for his last day."

Emmy came out of the house and shook her head.

"At least the killer wasn't in the house when you were."

"Emmy, dust the room the note was in for prints. Did you touch anything in the house?" he asked us.

"I touched the outside door handle, and the handle to his study. I probably touched the chair when I sat in it, too," I said.

"But you didn't touch the note?" he asked.

I shook my head. "I knew it was evidence."

"How about you, Marge?" he asked.

She bit her lip. "I started cleaning out the kitchen. It smelled horrible and food was going bad. But I've been in the house every week for decades, so you're going to find my prints all over the place. Do you think his killer was in the house?" Marge asked.

I gave her a hug. "Yes, of course the killer had been in the house. Who else would leave a note incriminating someone. But don't worry about it. We're going to catch him soon, and you'll never have to worry again. I promise."

She pulled away from me and looked at Connor. "What if it was a good Samaritan who wanted to remain anonymous? Lucas might be who we're looking for."

I supposed she had a point, but it was very unlikely. "We can go talk to him if you want."

Connor didn't like that at all. "No. You can't. I don't put any stock in this note, but it still needs to be checked out. Emmy and I will go talk to him and the two of you will go home. Go to the movies. Go for a walk by the pier. Do anything but investigate a murder. I don't want you talking to Bolen. Is that understood?"

I scowled at him, not answering.

"Go on, go do something else."

We got into my car and drove off. "Where are we going?" Marge asked.

I had a plan. If I could peek through a window and see Bolen while Connor was questioning him, I could read his thoughts. "We're going to Bolen's house to watch Connor question him."

"But Connor said—"

I scoffed. "He can't tell me not to do my job. And we won't be talking to him, I'll just be listening in on his thoughts."

Marge looked nervous. "Do you do that a lot? Listen to other people's thoughts?"

"Only for work. I don't listen to other people's thoughts regularly. I only get their random surface thoughts and unless they've been asked a direct question, it's pretty random in most people's minds."

She looked a little relieved.

"Oh, and I have a policy not to read my friends' thoughts. If you want me to know something, you'll tell me."

That finally erased the worry off her face. "Good. But I want to tell you this anyway. I keep thinking that if I hadn't insisted Randy go to you, and if you hadn't taken his case, he might still be alive. I was kind of blaming you for his death."

I drove past Bolen's house and turned down a side street so Connor wouldn't see us.

"I know it's not really your fault, but if I don't blame you, I have to blame myself," she said as she began to sob.

I pulled a wad of napkins from my armrest storage and handed them to her. "That's normal, honey. It's not true, but it's something everyone would think, at least for a little while."

She blew her nose and nodded. "And I can't thank you enough for sticking with the case. Once we've got the real killer to blame, I'll feel much better."

I gave her a small smile. "We all will. I want you to stay in the car—the fewer people skulking around the less likely we are to get caught."

She nodded again. "Make sure you get all the proof you need."

"If he's our guy, I will. I promise."

I got out of the car and crept through Mrs. Finkel's backyard. As children, we'd played in everyone's yards during summer break, and I knew a dozen different ways to get across the island without ever having to walk down a sidewalk. It was a handy skill to have if you knew your mother was out looking for you. My progress was halted by a relatively new box hedge. When had she planted that? There was a gap where the hedge hadn't yet met up with Mr. Levesque's hedge. I squeezed into the tiny space and peered through the leaves at the Bolens' backyard. No one was outside and the house seemed quiet. I couldn't see anyone looking out the windows, so I crept through the yard to stand under the kitchen window.

My heart was pounding. What if I got caught? Connor would be furious with me, but I had to know if Randy's death was connected to the case he'd hired me to solve. I could let Connor handle the whole thing, but that hurt my pride. I was a good investigator, even without telepathy, and I had a job to do.

I moved to the edge of the house and crouched down. I peered around the building and waited for Connor and Emmy to drive up. I was sure it would take them a while because they had to secure Randy's house and wait for a crime scene tech to arrive. Five minutes later, they finally arrived. Once I heard the front door shut, I felt bolder. As long as I barely poked my head above the bottom of the window, Connor wouldn't see me.

The only problem was that I had to circle the house and find which room they were in. With any luck, they'd move to the kitchen, where I'd be less likely noticed by the neighbors. I'd been training my telepathy to read thoughts at greater distances, but I'd had no luck with it when I couldn't see the person.

I stopped halfway down the house and peeked in the window, barely catching a flash of Connor's uniform walking to the back of the house. I turned and looked through the dining room window, but they weren't there. I continued to the kitchen window and saw them sitting at the table.

I had to stand on my toes to see in. Connor was focused on his questions and watching Lucas for any signs of deception. Lucas's thoughts were confused. He didn't understand why Connor was asking him about his friend's death.

Connor must have asked when Lucas had last seen Randy, because his thoughts switched to a poker game. Lucas, Randy, Pastor Bob, my father, and Joe Duncan sat around Lucas's dining room table. Beer cans littered the spaces between the players, and they were laughing at something. My father put his cards down, showing a pair of aces. His grin said he thought he'd won the pot, but Joe laid down his flush next. Everyone else threw their cards face down on the table as Joe pulled the chips toward his already large pile.

If that was really the last time Lucas saw Randy, he wasn't the killer. I lowered myself down to stand flat-footed and wiggle my aching toes. A voice asked, "Can I help you?" and I jumped.

Emmy had been watching me as I spied on the two men. "I can't believe the chief was right. I told him you wouldn't disobey a direct order like that. Now I have to buy him lunch. Thanks, Rebecca."

"Sorry about that. But he can't give me orders."

She smiled. "No, he knew you wouldn't listen to him. He wants you to call him and let him know what you found out, that's all."

She turned and left, leaving me confused. I thought I had the upper hand here, sneaking around so he wouldn't see me. Instead, he knew what I was going to do all along. I didn't like being so predictable. I needed to step up my game if I wanted to keep him guessing. He needed to learn the lesson to ask me to do things, not manipulate me into them.

Chapter 12

Despondent over having no suspects, I shuffled back to my car. If I could just get the entire island together and ask them all, "Did you kill Randy Petit?" and then look for the guilty thoughts, I'd have this case solved in no time. I wasn't sure I could listen to that many minds all at once, and I was sure I couldn't get everyone on the island together at once.

"Any luck?" Marge asked when I sat behind the wheel of my car.

I shook my head. "No. Well, yes, because now we know Bolen didn't kill your uncle. But no real luck, because we've got no suspects. And

Connor knew what we were going to do all along. He wants me to call him later to talk about what I saw."

"Seriously? You went to all that trouble to be sneaky and it was entirely unnecessary?"

I started the car. "Yup. I'm going to drop you back at my place. I need to talk to your other neighbors—Mamie and Janet. They may have seen something."

"Do you mind if I come with you? I need some things from my cottage and it would be a lot easier if I got them myself. I want to go back to work tomorrow, and I need to see my kids too."

"Of course you can. I'd be happy for the company, I just didn't want to bring you somewhere upsetting. That's all."

I put the car in drive and headed for Old Beach Path.

"If the crime scene tape is gone, you don't have to show me where he died, though. Okay? I may be living there for a while."

"Of course. Whatever you want." She sounded like she was accepting the idea that her uncle was dead and while she would mourn him for a long time, she had to start moving on with her life.

I parked in front of her cottage and winced at the graffiti. We needed to get that painted over as soon as possible. "Looks like the tape is gone, so you never need to know where it happened."

She got out and looked around. "Looks the same to me, or it will after a few coats of paint. I'll meet you back here when I'm done, but take your time talking to Janet and Mamie."

I got out of the car and walked to the farthest cottage, Mamie's. She and Lulu were about the same age, and I was impressed that they could live out here on their own. I was sure

Janet and Marge helped if they asked, but knowing stubborn Maine island women like I did, I doubted they ever asked.

I looked in the window as I walked to the door. Mamie was there, so I waved to her. Before I knocked, she opened the door. "Rebecca, is it?"

Mamie Knight didn't use a cane and had more energy than Lulu did. Her wiry hair hadn't gone all white yet either. "Yes. It's good to see you, Mrs. Knight."

"Lulu told me you'd be coming around to ask questions. Come on in, child, and I'll get you a drink."

Mamie's cottage was full to the rafters with furniture, books, and odd knickknacks from many decades. She had a writing desk in front of the window with a half-written letter on it. I wondered who she was writing to that she couldn't see on the island. In one corner was a dressmaker's form with a yellowing wedding dress on it.

I must have stared at the letter for too long, because she started talking about it. "I write to my grandchildren every week. My son took his family off the island when he couldn't get work as a pharmacist."

"I'm sorry, I didn't mean to be nosy," I apologized.

She poured a mug of tea and handed it to me. "Earl Grey. Sorry, I don't keep sugar or milk in the house." She motioned to the two leather reclining chairs in front of her television. "Sit down, make yourself at home."

"I was admiring all the things you have here. It's a curious mixture of old and new."

She sat next to me. "Mementos from a lifetime of experiences here. When I was younger, I traveled and saw a lot of the world, I never understood why my parents insisted that I visit foreign countries from the minute I graduated from high school. I wanted to go to college with my friends, but they said they'd only pay for my education if I spent time off the island first."

I nodded, thinking that was wise of them.

"Of course once I got home, I realized why I only had that small time to leave. I'm tied to the island now, but I'm grateful for the time I was away."

I took a sip of tea and relaxed into my chair. "I was admiring your wedding dress. I think it's a lovely tribute that you have it out on display rather than keeping it in a closet somewhere."

She smiled. "My daughter doesn't think so. She says I'm ruining it, letting it yellow in the light. It's too old fashioned and none of the girls in the family would want to wear it, so I do what I like. Every morning I see the dress, look up at the picture of my late husband, and tell him we're going to have a good day."

Her words stung. That was the kind of love I'd expected to have with George. Now it felt like he'd hurt me so badly I'd never be able to love someone that deeply again. "If you don't mind, I'd like to ask about the vandalism and if anything was stolen from your cottage."

She scoffed. "Just a bunch of kids who need more to do. The locks on these doors aren't hard to pick and half the island doesn't lock their doors anyway. The spray paint, though, that's different. Taking it up a notch like that worries me. What if they can't find what they're looking for? Will they start coming around when we're home, threatening us?"

I shuddered at the thought. Mamie was far too sweet a woman to be subjected to threats of violence. "I'm going to talk to the chief about this. Don't you worry about someone coming in and hurting you. If I have to, I'll stay and keep watch until we find out who's responsible."

She patted me on the knee. "You're a good girl. I think I have some old photos of your parents in here somewhere. Would you like to see them?"

I'd never seen photos of my parents before. Obviously, my father didn't photograph well, and my mother thought it was far too vain to hang photos of herself up in the house. "You do? Yes, please. I'd love to see them."

Mamie walked to a bookshelf on the other side of the room. As I followed her with my eyes, I realized she didn't have a bed. "Mrs. Knight, where do you sleep?"

She pointed to the chair she'd just got out of. "I sleep in the recliner. Put the legs out as far as they'll go and pull a blanket over me." She pulled a photo album off the bookshelf and turned back to me. "Don't feel bad for me. It keeps the lumbago away. I had a regular bed, but I kept pulling the muscles in my back. The doctor told me to use the recliner until I felt better, but why would I go back to the bed that hurt when I could sleep comfortably?"

Solid reasoning. "And you've got more space for anything else you want to keep."

I took the photo album from her hands and opened it. Each page had small, old-fashioned film photos of couples at their weddings.

"I was the church organist for over fifty years, and I took reception photos as well. Me and my trusty Kodak took photos for the Gazette. Keep going until you find your parents."

There were five photos on their page. My mother wore a severe white tea gown with a jewel neckline. She wore no jewelry and the dress had no lace, chiffon or bows. It looked unfinished, and if she dyed it black, it would have made a good mourning dress. My father wore a brown suit and scuffed leather shoes. The first photo was of my parents posing, smiling into the camera. The next was my parents with their parents. Both sets of parents had sour looks on their faces. I never thought my grandparents were upset by my parents' marriage, but the photo didn't lie.

The third photo was my parents' first dance. Dad held Mom closely, and she was beaming up at him. At least they were happy with each other then. The last two photos were of my mother and her bridesmaids and my father and his groomsmen.

"They looked very happy here. Could I take a picture of them?"

Mamie nodded her approval. "They were very much in love. Of course, no one wanted them to get married so young, but no one was willing to tell them why. I say someone should have told them why, given them a good reason to wait. But your grandparents . . . well, they'd never consider breaking the law, and their children paid the price for it."

I'd always wondered why my parents were together. I always thought my father was protecting my mother, but it turned out they had no idea what the future held in store for them. Had they waited to marry after they'd turned twenty-one, they might have realized my mother's love for everything outdoors and in a garden wouldn't have matched my father's need to avoid the sun at all costs. "Thank you for sharing these with me. I've never seen any of their wedding photos before."

I took a few close-up photos and put my phone back in my pocket. "Back to my reason for visiting today. Did you see anyone around the cottages? Particularly when they were spray-painted or when Randy was killed?"

"No. But I'm not home most days. I'm usually at the Senior Center. You should tell your mother to stop by. We've just had Ethel Mayberry drop out of our poker club, and we need another player."

I couldn't imagine my mother playing poker. She was always frugal to the point of making her life difficult. "I'll suggest it. And you're sure you didn't hear the shot? It could have sounded like a car backfiring."

"Like I told that nice chief, I didn't hear anything. I'm sorry I can't be more help."

I stood. "Would you like me to put this back?"

She nodded. "Yes, dear, if you would. Should I call if I see anything suspicious?"

"Call 9-1-1 immediately. They'll be able to get to you much faster than me."

I put the photo album away and took one more look around her cottage. "It was nice to talk to you. Thank you."

I took a deep breath of cold air and thought that Ellie, Marge and I would be a lot like Mamie when we were older. I could see us actively recruiting new, inexperienced players into our poker club to supplement our retirement income.

Marge was waiting at the car for me. "Anything?" she asked.

"Nothing about the case, no." I pulled out my phone and scrolled to the photos I just took. "She had photos of my parents' wedding."

Marge laughed. "They look so young!"

"Apparently they got married right out of high school. That's why my grandparents look so angry. Everyone wanted them to wait until after they were twenty-one."

Marge nodded. "Makes sense. Now that I think of it, my parents insisted on a long engagement. I never put it together before now."

"Do you want to talk to Janet with me or would you rather stay out here?" I asked.

Marge looked to the pink cottage and back to me. "Janet isn't here. I got bored waiting for you and knocked on her door. I figured I could talk to her and we could be done sooner. I don't want to be here after dark, you know?"

I could understand that. "Do you know where she works? We could talk to her there."

She shrugged. "Somewhere in town?"

"My mother might know. She seems to know just about everything else in town." As much as my mother had upset me since I'd been on the island, I was glad we were at least on speaking terms now.

My mother was raking the last of the leaves off the lawn when we drove up. She propped her rake against the house and hugged Marge. "Oh Marge, I'm so sorry for your loss. Randy was a good man."

"Thanks, Mrs. Wright. He was."

"Do you girls want to come in? It's getting chilly out here," my mother asked.

"Not now. We need to find Janet Cosgrave. Do you know where she works?"

"Janet? Sure. She's the bookkeeper at the grocery store."

Before she could ask any questions, I said, "Thanks mom. I'll call you later." I had to call and figure out a way to tell her I wouldn't be spending Thanksgiving at the house. Maybe I could promise Connor and I would stop by for dessert later on in the evening.

Shadow Island had one grocery store, the smallest Hannaford I'd ever seen. Over the years, each islander had picked a grocery shopping day and for the most part, stuck with it. My mother, for example, did her grocery shopping on Wednesday afternoon. She'd see friends, knew who would be working there, and it was more of a social event than shopping in a city, or even a town with more than one grocery store. Astute shoppers would notice when someone was buying groceries on a different day than normal and inquire if everything was okay with them.

Yes, we're that insular a community.

Marge and I walked into the Hannaford and smiled at the few raised eyebrows we noticed. The office was at the front of the store so we made a beeline for it. Janet looked up when we knocked on the locked door. Janet was about three years younger than Marge and me. Her dark hair showed a few strands of gray, and the three-tiered cotton skirt she wore was old and a little tight on her. Coordinating paisleys and florals hadn't been in style for a long time, but she still carried it off. She smiled when she opened the door and saw Marge standing behind me. I stepped to the side so Janet could hug Marge.

"I'm so sorry, honey. Are you doing okay?" Janet asked.

Marge nodded. "I think so. Do you have a minute to answer a few questions?"

Janet looked back at her desk. "Wait here for just a second." She went back to her desk, the door closing with a loud click of an automatic lock.

Once she'd cleared most of the papers off her desk, she opened the door for us. "Sorry about that, I know you're not here to steal the store's financial information, but I could get fired if I left anything out."

Marge smiled at her. "No problem. And we're sorry to bother you at work, it's just that Rebecca wants to double-check a few things with you about the break-ins at the cottages."

Janet motioned for us to sit. "Well, I'm not sure I can tell you anything I haven't already told the police, but ask away."

"Can you go through everything that you remember? Was anything taken from your cottage? Do you remember if you left your door unlocked?"

"Well, let's see. The first time, my back door wasn't closed properly. I don't use the door, and it's always shut tight. I didn't bother to lock the door, at least not until that day. Now it and the front door stays locked."

I nodded. “Do you remember what day this was?”

She squinted as she tried to recall. “It must have been two weeks ago now? Marge, do you remember what day it was?”

Marge shifted in her seat. “It was three weeks from Tuesday.”

“Three weeks! You’ve been living with this for three weeks?” I exclaimed.

“But he only broke in twice—”

“That you know about. What if the intruder has been there more often, and was just more careful?”

Marge looked down at her hands. “I didn’t think about that. At least not until the graffiti, and Randy.”

I looked to Janet. “Is anything missing from your cottage? Anything at all?”

“Nothing. I checked thoroughly, and the intruder didn’t take or leave anything.”

Just like the other cottages. I was frustrated with the lack of clues in this case. It seemed like the intruder was going in and out of cottages during the day, but neither Mamie nor Lulu saw anything. They weren't always at home , but they couldn't be counted on to be away at work like Marge and Janet. "Okay, thank you. One last question. Did you ever hear anything out of the ordinary? Someone in the trees behind the cottage or footsteps late at night?"

"No. But the waves can get loud during high tide, so I wouldn't have heard anything then. I'm sorry I wasn't more help."

Marge and I stood. "You have been helpful. If none of you heard or saw anything, that's important to know. It tells us that whoever we're dealing with is extremely cautious and may have done this sort of thing before."

Janet stood with us. "I'll keep an eye on your cottage until you're ready to come back, Marge."

Marge smiled at her. "Thanks, Janet. I shouldn't be away much longer."

As we walked out of the store, I sighed. "I'm not sure where to go next. We've got nothing to go on."

She stopped on the sidewalk. "I just had an idea. Do you think it might be one of the other residents? None of us would think twice seeing them around."

"I don't know," I said slowly, thinking about Janet, Mamie, and Lulu. "Lulu doesn't seem like she gets around that well. Mamie seems too nice, and Janet's at work all day. But what do you think? Do any of your neighbors seem like the type to wander around in your cottage?"

Marge started walking to my car. "No. But I'm not sure we've got any other ideas."

I unlocked my door and we climbed in. Before I started the car, my phone chimed with

Connor's ringtone, "Howlin' for You" by the Black Keys.

Marge rolled her eyes as she put the song and caller ID together. "A little on the nose, don't you think?"

"Hey Connor, what's up?"

CHAPTER 13

Connor wanted to take me to dinner for the second night in a row. I was sure that, even though he wanted to see me, he also wanted to keep tabs on my investigation. I had no problem telling him everything I'd learned, because it wasn't much. The trickier part was to get him to share what he'd learned.

Marge and I got back to my apartment, which had thoughtfully laid out an outfit for me to wear. Black pants, a green silk blouse, and an emerald necklace and set of earrings I was sure I didn't own. I picked up the necklace and squinted at the stone. I laughed at myself because

I wouldn't be able to tell if it was real or not. The teardrop shaped stone was large enough that it couldn't have been a real gem, but that didn't matter. It was beautiful no matter what its chemical composition.

The outfit and the jewelry were perfect, but every time my apartment arranged my life for me, I had to wonder. Did it have motives? Would I be better choosing my own outfits, cooking my own meals, and doing my own laundry? If nothing else, I was getting spoiled living here.

As I stepped out of my bedroom, Marge whistled at me. "You look fantastic. I didn't know you owned jewelry like that."

I gave her a wry smile. "I don't. The apartment picked out my clothes and this showed up with the rest of the outfit."

"Holy…" Marge said, "is Jack hiring, because I could use one of these luxury everything included apartments." She sighed.

"Imagine how much time I'd save if I didn't have to cook for the kids or do their laundry."

I sat next to her and put my earrings on. "You couldn't explain to them what was going on, though."

She bit her lip. "Yeah, okay, so I'll wait until they're old enough. Then I'll come work for Jack."

"I'm careful about who I bring up here. The apartment camouflaged itself into a tiny, little, disheveled one-room studio when George was here, but I think it wants its secret kept from most people." I could never explain it to anyone who didn't live on the island. What would happen if George came back and somehow saw the apartment in its usual large configuration? I wouldn't put it past him to try and talk me out of some alimony payments at least once or twice more, but I had to trust that an apartment that was sentient enough to know what I needed would be smart enough to know when he'd be coming back.

Marge laughed. "So your ex, who came to you for money, thinks you live in a dump? If he saw all this, he'd ask for twice the amount he wants."

She was right. I wouldn't put it past him to think I owed him something just because I was his ex.

Marge stood up. "Connor will be here soon, so let me get out of your way. I think I'll eat dinner, then see what's happening at the Horse. I don't really feel like being alone tonight."

My heart sank. I hadn't even asked Marge how she felt about my going out tonight. "Oh, I'm sorry. Do you want me to cancel? We can stay in and watch movies or something."

"No, thanks. You go on your date." She gave me an exaggerated wink. "I promise if I'm home, I'll be in my room when you get back. I'm looking forward to going out and talking to people like it's a normal night. It's exhausting being sad all the time."

She looked certain, so I didn't press her. Tonight's dinner was at Filet, the restaurant Connor's brother, Ian, owned. I was slowly ordering my way through the menu and hadn't found anything I didn't like yet. Tonight I'd try the smoked brisket with parmesan mashed potatoes.

I opened my door when Connor knocked and the first thing I saw was a dozen red roses. I took them from his hands and smiled. "They're beautiful. Come in while I get them in water."

I suspected that if I left the flowers on the kitchen counter, the apartment would take care of them for me. But like I said, I probably shouldn't get too spoiled living here. As it was, there was a pair of floral scissors and a vase of water waiting for me.

"Were you expecting flowers?" Connor asked.

I started to cut the stems to size. "No, but apparently the apartment was."

He sat on one of the kitchen stools. "I've lived on this island all my life, and I've seen a lot of weird things in my job, but this apartment has me stumped. I cannot figure out how it works."

I put the flowers in the vase. "I have no idea either. I'm not sure I should ask, so I'm just enjoying it while I can."

One bad thing about dating the police chief was that he knew when you were stretching the truth or hiding something from him. By the time our appetizers arrived, he was questioning me more like a suspect than a girlfriend.

"Spill it, Becks."

I had choices. I could tell him I was worried about Marge and still sad about Randy's death, or I could tell him how frustrated I was with my case. Both were true, but I thought that if I didn't tell him the whole truth, he'd know. "I've got two things on my mind. First, of course, Marge is in mourning and that makes me very sad. And of course I'm sad that Randy's gone too. But the thing that's most upsetting is that I cannot for the life of me figure out this case."

He set his fork down gently. "Which case?"

There was a right answer, and a wrong answer. He wanted me to say I was only looking into the break-ins, but that wasn't true. "Either. Both. I'm sure the break-in and the murder are related. I've spoken to everyone I can think of about the break-ins, and no one has any clue who would want to go in but not take anything."

I took a bite of my sweet potato crostini and continued. "Marge had an interesting idea today. She wondered if it wasn't one of the other women living out there. Maybe they were bored or needed to borrow a cup of sugar. She said she wouldn't think twice if she saw one of her neighbors near another of the cottages."

"I thought of that, but I can't see it. If I don't get a break in the case soon, I'll have to look at the four of them as suspects."

"Four? You can't possibly think Marge is behind the break-ins. And she'd never kill anyone, much less her uncle," I said, shocked he would consider her a suspect.

"I can't rule someone out just because they're my friend. That's not how policing works," he said.

Ian arrived with our dinners. We'd both chosen the same dinner, but he only brought out one plate of brisket. "I know you wanted brisket, but I need you to try this bourbon-glazed salmon and let me know what you think."

The salmon looked delicious. "I'm going to make you come running with me in the mornings if you keep feeding me like this," I threatened him.

"Oh no. I'm up at the crack of dawn to start work. No time for exercise other than what I get here," Ian said. "Make Connor go with you."

"I get enough exercise chasing kids around town," Connor said.

After Ian left, I asked about the kids. "Do you really chase kids down? What's going on?"

He took a bite of the salmon. "Try this. It's incredible."

I took a bite and he was right. The bourbon was set off with honey, ginger and soy and I could have eaten the whole piece myself. Instead, I went back to my question. "The kids?"

Connor frowned. "We've got no leads on the spray paint. Stores on the mainland keep their spray paint locked up so they can monitor who buys it, but they don't do that at Island Hardware. No one there recalled selling black spray paint recently, so I focused on kids. It's gotten me nowhere though."

I grinned. "Sure it has, you've done more running this week. That can't be all bad."

He chuckled. "It's not. You should see their faces when I skip their shortcuts to use better ones we made decades ago. I meet them where they're going and they can't figure out how."

"So you've got no worthwhile leads either?" I asked.

"It pains me to say it, but I don't. Not unless you heard something interesting when I was questioning Lucas Bolen."

I took a sip of wine before answering. "I didn't. The last time he saw Randy was at a poker game. The other players were Pastor Bob, my father, and Joe Duncan. Lucas didn't have any angry or bitter memories that I could see, and as much as he and Randy argued, Lucas genuinely liked Randy. I don't think he's our guy."

"I don't either, but it's good to have corroboration." He reached out and took my hand in his. "I wish we had someone like you on the force. We could cut through so much wasted time and effort with a simple scan of a suspect's thoughts."

"Once people realized what was happening, the uproar would be catastrophic. Laws aren't written to keep telepaths from scanning people, and it poses a genuine threat to someone's right to be judged for what they do, not what they think."

Connor closed his eyes for a moment. "I know. It's wishful thinking, and if I were you I wouldn't tell many people what you can do, or you'll find you have very few friends. Yours is a talent people are afraid of."

He let go of my hand and took a bite of my potatoes. "Speaking of being afraid of you, have you heard from George since he left the island?"

I shook my head. "No. He called Kelsey, though, and told her my apartment is a dump."

Connor looked confused. "What kind of mansion did you have in Boston?"

"No mansion, just a large house in an expensive neighborhood. Troy Torres's new house will probably be about the same size as mine was."

Connor was flabbergasted. "That house is huge. Way too much for the island and if you ask me, he's overcompensating for something."

I smirked. "Could be. I know George was. But the apartment shrunk itself down to a one-room studio, threw my dirty laundry around, and didn't do any of the dishes. Is it weird to think the apartment knew what George needed to see?"

He shrugged. "You'll have to ask Jack. I've got no idea how that building works. You're not tempted to cut back on your alimony, are you? From what I've seen, you've earned every cent, no matter how much it is, for putting up with him for so long."

I laughed. "You're right about that. I'm not giving anything back. Especially after he chose to use his kids to try and manipulate me." I took a sip of wine. "And you know what really bothers me? When I asked for a part-time nanny to help me with Kelsey, he laughed at me, told me that if I wasn't going to contribute to the household that the least I could do was raise our child."

Connor set his jaw in anger. "He'd better not come back to the island. If I see him again, we'll have a come-to-Jesus moment where I will make sure he realizes how much he never deserved you."

"I don't think he'll be back. I'm sure his financial problems are temporary. His boss is upset that he divorced me and he withheld the bonuses George had planned on getting. By the time the next quarter comes around, his boss will have forgotten all about me, or Chloe will have charmed him, and George will be back to making his regular bonuses."

"I could talk to him now. Or I could have someone from Boston have a word."

I shook my head. "No. Don't. He gave it a shot and failed. He won't try again."

I cut into my brisket and took a bite. "You're lucky you're so cute, otherwise I might have to ask Ian to marry me for his cooking alone."

"You don't want to do that. He's married to his work. You'd never see him, I know I never do."

"Yeah, right," I smirked. "Like you're not completely devoted to your work too. And speaking of which, I have questions."

He furrowed his brow at me. "You do? About my work?"

I took a bite of my potatoes. "For potatoes like these, I may not need to ever see him."

Connor ate a forkful of my potatoes. "I see what you mean."

"I wanted to ask about the shifters in your cells. Do they just show up and lock themselves in? Are they okay in there? How long do they have to go through all that? And how do you separate people so they don't hurt each other?"

"There's a lot of shifters on the island, but not all of them are dangerous. You remember Emmy, the bunny shifter officer?"

I nodded. She'd used her ability to sneak past a booby-trapped door and defuse a bomb.

"She didn't spend a minute in the cells. Her parents were able to keep her at home. It's better that way, but the larger animals, and the more vicious ones like dogs and wolves, need to be kept locked up. It keeps them safe, and everyone safe from them until they're in control.

One person per cell, and we try to have an empty cell between them too."

"Do they get . . . did you get to choose what animal you changed into?"

He frowned. "No. Just like you didn't get to choose telepathy. It takes most people about four months to get control of themselves, but they're welcome in the cells at any time, no matter how long they've been shifting. Why are you asking me all these questions?"

"My parents haven't told me anything, and they're still upset because they think I didn't fight hard enough to keep George. So I don't know much at all about how anyone's powers work on the island."

He sighed and took my hand. "The real truth of the matter is no one knows. Anyone who thinks they know why some people aren't chosen or why the chosen get the powers they do is lying. No one wants to admit they don't know, so they cling to any pattern they think they see."

I nodded. "Uncertainty is a bitch. But my parents could have at least told me something might happen. Maybe then I wouldn't have fallen down the stairs and wound up in the hospital."

"How old is your daughter?" he asked.

I finished the last of my wine. "Kelsey's nineteen. But she's never been on the island. My parents made sure of that. I shouldn't have to tell her anything."

"What if it isn't the island? What if it's the families who live here? Do you really want her to be as shocked as you were when you found out?"

He had a good point. "No. By this logic then, either the twins or Kelsey may have a surprise in their future."

Connor nodded. "And there's nothing we can do about it, either."

"Has the town never had anyone study what's going on here? I can't believe the entire town is willing to live ignorance."

Ian came out with our desserts. He placed an entire tray of one-bite confections in front of us. He handed Connor a sheet of paper with a picture of each dessert on it and a pen. “If you wouldn’t mind doing some market research for me and letting me know which you like best, dinner’s on the house.”

Ian was always coming up with different ways to make sure our meals were free. I think it was his way of showing how happy he was that we were dating again.

Connor took the paper and pen. “You can buy our drinks for the research, but we pay for the rest ourselves.”

Ian left, mumbling something about not being able to pay a bill that was never presented.

Each item on the tray was a perfect miniature version of a larger confection. There was pumpkin pie, crème brûlée, tiramisu, an éclair, and a dozen others that I couldn’t wait to try. “What should we start with?” I asked.

"Cheesecake is first on the list," Connor said.

I took my fork and gently broke it in two. I fed him half, then ate the other myself. Even though I had just a half a mouthful of dessert, I could taste all the flavors of an entire piece of cheesecake. The graham cracker crust, the cream cheese, even the little bit of cherry topping came through. "This must be some kind of magic."

We finished our desserts and were hard-pressed not to give each one a ten out of ten score. We tried to flag a waitress down to get our bill, but neither would approach our table. In the end, Connor left a hundred-dollar bill on the table. "That'll teach him not to let us pay."

As we walked out, I was confused. "If we give him more money, how will that help?"

"Dinner wasn't that expensive. If he wanted to save us money, his plan backfired. We paid too much."

I still wasn't sure I understood. "This must be a sibling thing."

He opened his truck door for me. Before I got in, I put my arms around him and pulled him close. "Thank you for dinner. I love how we can sit and talk about anything and be comfortable with each other."

Connor put his hands on my waist. "This must be a married person thing. Why wouldn't we be comfortable talking with each other?"

I blew out a breath. "It happens. Some couples just run out of things to say to each other."

He pulled me closer. The woodsy smell of his aftershave filled my nose. I looked from his eyes to his lips, then back to his eyes. Slowly, he lowered his lips to mine and I felt them curve into a smile. "Let's never run out of things to say," he whispered.

I would have stood there kissing him until the sun rose, but he stepped back and helped me into the truck. I grinned all the way back to my apartment. I didn't compare Connor to George often, but the George I was married to was nothing compared to Connor.

On the drive home, Ellie called, asking me to stop by her work.

"Sure thing, what's up?" I asked.

"I don't know. I want you to come take a look at something for me," she said.

"Okay. I'm on my way home now. I'll change and be right over."

"Where are you going?" Connor asked

"Ellie asked me to go to the Horse. She wants me to look at something," I explained.

"I can't go with you. I've got to get to the cells. I've got a couple guys coming in for the first time and they'll need some help," he said.

I loved that he spent so much of his time taking care of other shifters. I wished each different talent had someone to guide them. Even I could use help sometimes, and I was sure there was more I could learn about my telepathy except that I had no one to teach me. "That's fine. I'll change and take my car."

"Not what I meant. I can wait for you to change and then drop you off. I don't want you going anywhere alone at night until this murderer is found."

True to her word, Marge was in her room when we got to my apartment. I changed quickly into jeans and a sweater, took off the jewelry I was wearing, and slipped on a pair of leather boots.

Before I left, I knocked on her door. "Just wanted to let you know I was going to the Horse to talk to Ellie. I won't be out late."

"Great. Maybe I'll see you there later," she said from behind the door.

I thought it must be scary to change into an entirely different creature during the full moon, especially when you most likely didn't have any family members who could tell you what to expect. It was scary enough becoming a telepath, and I didn't have painful bodily changes to go through, just vertigo. And that was only because I wasn't living on the island.

The entire supernatural system of the island needed a good overhaul. Rather than let people figure out what was happening to them as it happened, I thought we needed a series of meetings with our twenty-year-olds to explain what they could expect in the next year. Parents weren't always doing a good job, partly because they only had experience with their own power. Imagine a telepath like me trying to explain how to be a mermaid to my daughter—I couldn't possibly do it justice. And if both parents had no abilities, they couldn't explain anything to their children at all.

That was it—we needed an introductory course and then a mentorship program. I had to speak to the mayor about this. As soon as I found

Randy's killer I would make an appointment to see Gene Haskins.

CHAPTER 14

I walked into the Horse and was surprised to see how crowded it was for a weeknight. A table of construction workers, including Yann and Joe, raised their beer bottles to salute me. I smiled and gave them a little wave. As I pushed my way up to the bar I realized there were very few women in the room. Was it men's night? Was that even a thing, or were most nights men's night in a bar?

Ellie made her way over to me. "Thanks for coming. What can I get you?"

I had no idea what I wanted. "You choose. Make it weak, though, I've got a lot of work to do tomorrow."

She grinned at me. "I know just the thing. Wait here."

I stood and as I waited, more and more men began to notice me. Was this going to become an issue? I looked around for the bouncer and relaxed when I saw who it was. Paul Hemming was one of the largest men I knew who wasn't an actual giant. He also had five sisters and I knew I'd be safe with him watching the room.

He gave me a short nod and I peeked into his thoughts. As I expected, he was focusing on the crowd and keeping them from getting overly rowdy.

"Try this, Becks. I think you'll like it," Ellie said.

My drink looked like a seltzer mixed with grenadine and a maraschino cherry on top. I took a sip and was surprised to taste a bit of vodka. Enough to make the drink for adults only, but not enough to keep me from driving home. "It's good. What is it?"

"It's a Dirty Shirley, only I put half the usual vodka in it. I know what a lightweight you are," Ellie said.

She wasn't wrong. "Why did you want to see me tonight?"

"Adam Krawczyk was in here earlier, boasting about a huge inheritance he was about to get. You missed him, though, because Paul had to see him out. Adam usually nurses one or two beers for the entire night, but tonight he was throwing them back and he wasn't handling it well."

Herbert was flat broke and I couldn't imagine what kind of inheritance Adam thought he was going to get. "Weird. Did Herbert own something I didn't know about?"

Ellie shrugged. "Not that I know of. I wish you'd gotten here sooner, because you could have taken a look and seen what he was talking about. I'm dying of curiosity."

I took another sip of my drink. I didn't think I needed to read Adam's thoughts. "I'll look into Herbert tomorrow at the office. We've got some pretty impressive databases and now you've got me curious too."

"Thanks, Becks," she said as she walked off to serve more customers.

I turned my back to the bar and took my time finishing my drink, watching the crowd and looking to see who sat together and who avoided each other. Jack read the paper from cover to cover every week to keep an eye on what was happening in town, but I could learn just as much by seeing who drank together.

It was a good sign the construction crew were all at the same tables they'd pushed next to each other. They worked together every day and if they wanted to spend their off time together, too, then either they liked each other or they were united in despising their boss. Maybe a little of both. If I had the chance to see Troy with them tonight I'd be able to tell.

Marge walked in and looked around. Before she could walk to me, one of her friends at the Gazette waved her over to their table. Every person at the table, even the editor, stood and hugged her. One of the reporters whose name I hadn't learned yet brought her a margarita. Marge looked back at me and shrugged.

I shrugged back. She could join me later if she wanted. I was happy to stand here and watch people.

Bruce Morrigan, the bar's owner, tapped me on the shoulder. "Do you want a seat?" he yelled over the noise.

I'd been standing long enough that sitting down sounded good. "Where?" I asked.

He pointed to a small table with a reserved sign on it. Reserved? The Horse was a semi-seedy working-class bar. No one ever reserved tables. I picked up an extra napkin from the bar and joined him at the table. "Thanks," I yelled just before the noise of the room fell away.

My eyes widened. "Did you do that?"

He grinned at me. "Sure did. It's the handiest talent to have if you run a bar. I never have to strain to hear anyone with this cone of silence around me." He looked at my glass. "Let me get you another."

Between the wine at dinner and the drink I'd already finished, I didn't want more alcohol. "Thanks. Tell Ellie less vodka, please." I hoped she knew I meant no vodka.

Bruce waved to Ellie and made some complicated hand gestures she seemed to understand. "That's not sign language, is it?"

He chuckled. "No. It's just something that's evolved over time. I see that Connor's not with you tonight. You're not having trouble, are you?"

Nice try. "No. He's got things to do at the station tonight and Ellie asked me to stop by."

He cocked an eyebrow. "She did?"

"Yeah, Adam Krawczyk was acting weird, she said, and she wanted me to see him."

"So you could read his mind?" Bruce asked.

I said nothing for a moment. I wasn't sure how he'd learned what my ability was.

"Don't worry, Becks, your secret is safe with me. You'd be surprised what people tell their local bartender. I'm pretty sure I know the talent of just about everyone on the island."

I perked up. That could be very useful if my ideas to help younger people with their talents were approved by the mayor. "Oh. So who blabbed mine?"

He looked away then back to me. "I'd rather not say. He was really drunk, and I doubt he even remembers telling me."

That was all I needed to know. There were only four men on the island who knew what I could do—Jack, Connor, Officer Breen, and my father. I'd bet everything my father was in here one night and told Bruce more than he should have.

Ellie came by with our drinks. "I'm off in a half hour, boss. That okay with you? We're still busy and I can stay if you need me."

"I can handle it, Ellie. Thanks."

Bruce and I spent the next half hour catching up on the last twenty-five years. He'd been married once, but divorced when his wife decided she wanted someone who wasn't out all hours of the night working. I told him about George and Kelsey. He loved the photos of Kelsey and agreed that George was an ass.

Before I knew it, Ellie and Marge were back at the table. "Ready to go?" Ellie asked.

I finished my drink, which thankfully had no vodka in it, and stood. "It's been great catching up, Bruce. Have a good night."

The three of us walked out into the cold November air. I'd gotten used to the quiet in Bruce's cone of silence, but even outside the bar was noisy. "Connor doesn't want us walking home. He's worried the streets aren't safe."

Marge jingled her car keys. "He might be right. I'll drive."

I snatched the keys from her. "I saw them buying you drinks, I'll drive."

She grabbed them back from me. "And I saw Bruce buying you a drink, too. Don't think I wasn't keeping an eye on you two. He was looking very happy to have your attention."

"What?" I sputtered. "We were just catching up, and my second drink had no booze in it at all. Tell her, Ellie."

Ellie grabbed the keys and jammed them in her pocket. "I'm driving. We're going to Beck's apartment because you two have been investigating something and you need to fill me in."

Neither Marge nor I argued with Ellie, mostly because we didn't want to fish the keys out of her pocket. My apartment had set Connor's roses in the middle of the dining room table, along with a pot of coffee and a late night snack of chocolate chip cookies.

"How did you know we were investigating?" Marge asked Ellie.

Ellie rolled her eyes. "I'm a bartender. I hear everything that's going on in town."

"Okay, great. What do you know about who killed Randy?" I asked.

Ellie looked surprised. "Nothing. That's not the kind of thing I'd keep to myself. You don't believe I wouldn't call Connor as soon as I could, do you?"

Oops. I hadn't meant to offend my friend. "No, of course not. I thought maybe you heard rumors, you know, the kind of thing you might not believe was true."

"Still nothing. Sure, everyone talked about him for a day, but no one had any idea who would have killed him." She smiled. "I heard some really wild stories about him when he was younger though. He took some amazing risks and it all panned out for him."

Marge nodded. "He was a seer, so they weren't really risks."

Ellie's eyes widened. "That makes a lot more sense. So tell me what you've got so far."

I poured myself a cup of coffee, hoping it was decaf. "We've got a whole lot of nothing right now. We've cleared a lot of people, and now we've got no leads whatsoever. Nothing for the murder, and not even anything for the break-ins."

Marge frowned. "We're down to interrogating Lulu and Mamie for breaking in to borrow a cup of sugar."

Ellie leaned back in her chair. "Yeah, that's about as nothing as you can get. I was going to ask my father-in-law about Adam tomorrow morning. Want to come along? At least that'll be a mystery we can solve."

Ellie's father-in-law was Elden Fine, president of the Shadow Island Bank. If Herbert had money, it would either be stuffed in his mattress or, more likely, in the bank. "I'm game. But will he tell you?"

"He won't be able to tell us much, but he can give us a vague impression of whether the amount he has in his accounts would be worth bragging about in a bar."

"Good enough," Marge said. "We can figure that out, then get back to our regularly scheduled investigation. But can we go first thing? I'd like to get to work by noon. As much as I love this apartment, I need to get back to some semblance of my normal life."

"Absolutely," Ellie said. "If you don't mind, I'll drive your car home, then pick you up at eight."

We said good night to Ellie, then tidied up the coffee and cookies.

As I lay in bed waiting to fall asleep, I thought it seemed like a waste of time to see what Adam was bragging about. On the other hand, at least we'd start the day solving a mystery.

Chapter 15

Ellie picked us up at eight, and we were all oddly excited to get to the bank when it opened. The apartment hadn't made us any breakfast, so we decided to go to the diner.

"Maybe Frankie can tell us something," Ellie suggested.

I wasn't sure she'd have time to gossip during the breakfast rush, but we could ask.

The three of us squeezed into a booth made for two and Frankie brought us coffee right away. "Be with you as soon as I can. This rush can't go on for much longer," she said.

Connor's mother was seated at a table on her own. "Girls, why don't you take my extra chair?"

Marge, who was squeezed in next to me, stood and took it. "Thanks."

We'd finished our coffee before Frankie had time to make it back to us. I was eyeing the glass domed pastry stand on the counter and considering helping myself just to save her time and energy. She could write up our order when we were done eating.

I was working up my nerve when Mayor Haskins took the last seat at the counter, in front of the danishes. So much for my brilliant self-serve strategy.

Marge looked at her watch. "What time does your father-in-law get to work, Ellie? It's already eight twenty."

I looked for Frankie, who was still hustling food to tables as fast as she could.

"Maybe we should go to the bank first, then come back for breakfast when it's not so busy."

Ellie picked up her empty mug, looked disappointed that it hadn't magically refilled itself, then put it down again. "He's already there. He comes to the diner most mornings for coffee and a muffin, and I thought it would be less suspicious looking if we ran into him rather than barge into his office and ask what Adam was going to inherit."

Marge and I shushed her. "Do you want the whole town to know what we're doing?" I asked.

"It's so loud in here, I doubt anyone heard us," she said.

"I heard you," Connor's mother said. "What are you girls up to?"

"Just a little fun," I said. "Adam was at the Horse last night bragging about a huge inheritance he was getting. We wanted to see if it was true."

"He was probably lying. He's always been trouble. Did you know he uses his talent to take advantage of other people," she said.

I was sure he wasn't the only person on the island who did this, but in such an insular community word got around fast and islanders had long memories. Screw someone over and it was likely no one would trust you for decades to come.

"How does he do it?" Ellie asked.

"He's a shifter, only he can take the shape of anyone, or anything he wants," Connor's mother said. In high school, Connor's parents insisted I call them Mom and Dad, and they were the positive parenting role models I used when raising Kelsey. I wish I felt comfortable calling her Mom again, but I didn't. On the other hand, Mrs. Dougherty seemed far too formal.

"No way! I've never heard of that ability before," Marge said.

Connor's mother nodded. "Thankfully there aren't many on the island. Adam is the only one I know about."

Frankie brought Mrs. Dougherty her breakfast. I looked with envy at her scrambled eggs and toast. "I'll get to you as soon as I can, ladies," Frankie said as she rushed by us.

I turned back to my table and spoke to Ellie. "Okay, as soon as we talk to your father-in-law, I've got to get back to my real case."

The mayor stood and left, leaving my path to pastry open.

I got up and took three pastries from the stand. We didn't have plates so I grabbed extra napkins. "We're all having danishes and we'll pay Frankie later. We've got to get a move on."

Before we were finished scarfing down breakfast, Elden Fine walked in and took the seat vacated by the mayor. I was glad I grabbed food as quickly as I did. "Should you go talk to him?" I asked Ellie.

"Hey, Dad," she called over the noise of the diners.

He looked around and smiled at Ellie. He started to yell back but decided to stand near us instead. "Good morning, Ellie. I don't see you here very often."

"I like to sleep in if I worked late the night before. But this was the only time I could have breakfast with Marge and Becks. Plus, I wanted to come see you in your office. We have a question about banking."

The corners of his mouth turned down. "I'm sorry, I can't. I've got a meeting on the mainland, and as soon as I get Frankie to wrap me up a muffin, I'm headed to the ferry. I'll be in the office all day tomorrow, though. Why don't you come see me then?"

I was disappointed. Talking about Adam and his odd conviction he was coming into money was my one distraction for the day. After that, I had to focus on finding Randy's killer. I gestured to our table. "We couldn't wait any longer, so I grabbed breakfast while she was waiting on other tables. Why don't you grab something and we'll put it on our bill. The ferry is going to leave in ten minutes, and you don't want to miss it."

"I suppose in desperate times," he said. "Thank you. And I'll pay you back tomorrow when you come to see me." He took two muffins and left quickly.

"Well that sucks. I might as well head into the office," Marge said.

"Yeah, I should get to work too," I agreed. "Sorry we couldn't figure this out for you, Ellie."

I took a piece of paper from the small notebook I kept in my bag and wrote a note to Frankie explaining what we were paying for and that she should keep the change for her tip.

We threaded our way through the full diner to the door. As Marge pushed the door open, Elden Fine held it for us to leave. "Ladies," he said.

He had no muffins in his hands, and he hadn't been gone long enough to eat one, never mind both of them. "Dad?" Ellie said.

He beamed at her. "Good morning. What are you doing here?"

Ellie, Marge, and I looked at each other, then back to Fine. "You were just here. You're going to miss your ferry if you don't hurry up," Ellie said.

"What are you talking about? I've been in my office all morning. And I'm not going to the mainland for another few weeks," he said.

Why would Adam disguise himself as the bank president? There was only one reason I could think of—he was going to rob the bank. "You should go back to your office and stay there," I said. "I think you're about to be robbed."

We rushed out, scanning the street for the other Elden Fine, who was probably Adam in disguise.

Chapter 16

Marge pointed down the street, away from the ferry and the bank. "There he is!"

We matched his pace until no one was between us and him. "Are we ready to run?" I asked. "We need to grab him before he disappears and turns into someone else."

Marge and Ellie nodded. I was grateful we were past the age where we felt high heels were necessary.

We started running, and it wasn't long before he realized we were after him. He turned back to see us and ran into Bonnie Chevalier. "Stop him," I yelled to her.

She looked confused but did her best to hold him where he was. He pushed her out of the way, and she stumbled and hit her head on the ground.

"I've got her," Marge said. "You go on."

Ellie and I continued to chase Elden/Adam and I had a moment of doubt. What if this was the real Elden and man currently at the diner was the fake? I discarded the thought. Innocent men didn't run from middle-aged women walking down the street.

He was pulling away from us and I resolved to add speed drills to my workouts. Ellie was panting behind me. "I'll catch up," she said as I kept chasing him.

He turned into the alley between the grocery store and the florist. I followed him in, surprised he'd stopped running. "Adam, just stop." I said as I tried to catch my breath. "I'm sure we can work all this out."

He advanced on me, lightning fast, and pushed me up against the wall. "It's too late now. You've ruined everything."

Elden Fine was a happy, kind man and it was strange to hear anger from him. "No, it's not. I have a lot of sway with the chief, you know I can talk to him for you. Just explain to me what's going on."

That was the wrong thing to say, because he punched me. My head snapped to the side and scraped across the brick wall. My vision darkened for a moment then cleared. I think he expected me to fall to the ground, but there was no way I was going to let him get away. I grabbed onto him and held myself up. The metallic taste of blood filled my mouth and I spat.

Adam looked horrified at the blood staining his shirt. "Jesus! You can't just spit blood at people. That's assault." He broke my grip on his shirt and hit me again, this time in the abdomen.

That punch didn't hurt nearly as much. I straightened up, stepped back and made a fist. I couldn't have looked threatening, because he looked down at my fist and laughed. "You're such a girl! If you hit me like that, you'll break your thumb."

I untucked my thumb and swung. The look of shock on his face as my fist connected with his nose was glorious. Blood ran from his now broken nose and I thought that if I didn't manage to keep him here until my friends arrived, at least I'd landed a good hit.

He wrapped his hand around my throat and began to squeeze. I clawed at his hand but I couldn't dislodge his grip.

My vision dimmed again, and I thought I could use a good nap. In the distance, I thought I could hear Connor yelling my name, but that couldn't be. He didn't know where I was. Everything was growing murky and indistinct in my head, which is why I wasn't so concerned when the man in front of me took on my appearance, swelling jaw, scraped face and all.

"I'm in here, Connor," my voice said as my doppelganger released his hold on me. "I've got him."

I sank to the ground, wanting to yell that I was the real Rebecca, but my assailant gave me one sharp kick to the ribs and I needed to focus on breathing without passing out.

I watched as Adam ran from the alley into Connor's arms, crying about how badly he'd been hurt. I struggled to stand but couldn't until Officer Breen assisted me. "That's not me," I rasped. "You never dropped him off at the library to do research with Jack."

Breen's eyes widened and he looked to Connor. Breen gave a tiny shake of his head and almost instantaneously, Connor had my double in handcuffs.

I sagged against Breen and he held me up until the paramedics arrived. Getting onto the stretcher was the most painful thing I'd ever endured, including childbirth. Every motion felt like I was jabbing knives into my lungs, my face, or my brain. "Okay, Miss Wright, lean back and we'll be done moving you," the EMT said.

I closed my eyes and tried to will away the pain.

"Just let me take a look at you," he said, "and we'll have you fixed up in no time."

Starting with my torso, I felt a warm, soothing wave penetrating my skin and moving upward. As the wave passed, I realized my ribs didn't hurt anymore. I opened one eye to see the EMT, whose nametag read Rothman, grinning at me. "Give me a few more minutes and you'll be fully healed."

I closed my eye again and let him finish working on me.

"Okay, you're all set now," he said.

I felt my ribs as I opened my eyes. I had no pain at all. My jaw didn't feel swollen and I couldn't taste blood anymore. "Wow, thanks," I said lamely.

"Let's get you up and you can tell the chief what really happened," Breen said. "The other person who looks like you keeps insisting you lured him into the alley and beat him up."

I slowly swung my legs off the stretcher and stood up. Breen and Rothman had their arms out to support me if I needed them, but I didn't. I took a cautious, deep breath and when that didn't hurt, I strode out of the alley to Connor.

"Becks?" he asked.

I smiled. "It's me."

Adam was sitting in the back of Connor's cruiser yelling that I was a liar. "Connor! We went to the prom together. I can't believe you can't tell the real me."

There was so much Adam didn't know about our relationship that I could use to prove my identity, he didn't stand a chance. "Last night you offered to have someone from Boston tell George to leave me alone."

He breathed a sigh of relief. "Thank god. If that"—he pointed to Adam—"was the real you, I was going to rethink my life choices."

I laughed. "He is seeming a little shrewish."

Marge and Ellie burst through the police cordon. "Are you . . . you?" Marge asked.

I nodded. "Yes, and that's Adam in the cruiser."

With my friends flocked around me, Adam gave up and resumed his own form. I was amazed to see how off-kilter his nose was. I must have landed a great hit.

"Hey, Chief," Rothman said, "now that he's back to his natural form, can I bandage him up?"

Connor nodded. "But don't waste your ability on him. He'll be fine with regular medicine, and you already look exhausted."

Connor was right. Rothman had dark circles under his eyes, and I thought I could see the beginnings of bruising on his neck. "Did he take all my injuries?" I asked. If so, he must be in a lot of pain.

"Yes, but he doesn't feel them all. If he pushed himself to heal Adam, he would," Connor said. "I don't have a good handle on what happened here. Do you feel up to coming to the station and questioning our suspect with me?"

I grinned. "Absolutely. I'm not entirely sure what was going on either. I think he was planning a bank robbery, but I'm not clear on how."

We waited for Rothman to put splints in Adam's nose and disinfect the scrapes on his hands and arms before we headed to the station.

Connor and I drove to the station and Breen took Adam to be booked.

"What were you doing there? How did you know I was in trouble?" I asked.

"My mother called me. She said something hinky was going on with Elden Fine, and that there seemed to be two of him. She said you rushed out of the diner, and she was afraid you were in danger."

I chuckled, amazed it didn't hurt. "Hinky? Like what they say in Scooby-Doo?"

He smiled. "I think that was jinkies. Hinky is from The Fugitive. We saw both a million times, though, because she raised us on the classics."

"I'll have to call and thank her for looking out for me." If he hadn't shown up, I wasn't sure what would have happened to me.

We met Breen in processing, where he handed Connor a clear bag of things that looked like they came from Adam's pockets. "I arrested him for assault and told him we have further charges pending."

Connor looked at the items in the bag. "Thanks, Alex. Bring him to interrogation when he's done here."

Connor walked me to the interrogation room and Breen brought Adam in a minute later. Breen locked Adam to the interrogation table and left.

Connor turned the tape recorder on. "Adam Krawczyk, you've been arrested for aggravated assault on Miss Wright. You've been read your rights and those still hold. For the tape, do you want an attorney at this time?"

Adam shook his head. "No. Look at me. She beat me up, I was just defending myself. You've got no case and I'm going to love every minute of suing the both of you for this miscarriage of justice."

I suppose if you'd already been arrested, you didn't have anything to lose by trying to bluster your way out of the situation. Connor put the bag of Adam's possessions on the table. I hadn't taken a good look at what was in the bag, but I noticed when Adam's eyes homed in on a small key. Key for a storage space lock? Gym locker key? No, it was a safe-deposit key.

"You're looking at fifteen years already, why not make it easy on yourself and cooperate," Connor said soothingly.

But Adam wasn't buying it. He sat back and said nothing.

"What's in the safe-deposit box?" Connor asked. "And whose box is it?"

"It's mine," Adam said.

Connor frowned. "You don't have two nickels to rub together, and neither did your uncle. So why were you bragging about an inheritance last night at the Horse?"

"Wasn't me. Must have been someone else."

Connor scoffed. "It was a full bar last night. I can get two dozen people to confirm it was you." He turned to the two-way mirror and said, "Breen, come here for a moment."

Breen walked in and Connor gave him the safe-deposit key. "Ask whose key this is at the bank. If they give you any trouble, tell them they were about to be robbed and this was the target."

I wondered if the bank was allowed to give out information on who owned safe-deposit boxes. Then again, earlier this morning we were going to ask some questions I was fairly sure Ellie's father-in-law shouldn't have answered.

"What I don't understand is how you could go into this job so unprepared. You pretend to be the bank president, but don't even do any simple reconnaissance to see what his schedule is like. Even I know he goes to the diner every morning for breakfast. You could have picked anyone else and you might not have been caught."

"I did," Adam started to explain.

I held my breath, waiting for him to say more, but he didn't.

"You did? So you were someone else first, but had to change into the bank president? Why?"

Breen returned and handed a folded piece of paper to Connor. Connor opened it up and then showed me. "Was this person at the diner this morning?"

I nodded. The mayor sat right in front of the pastries shortly after we got to the diner. He left, though. My eyes widened with the realization that he left right after Ellie blabbed our plans for the morning, and not more than a couple minutes later Adam walked in, looking like her father-in-law.

"I've got it figured out," I said.

Connor raised an eyebrow.

"Adam was in the diner twice this morning. First he looked like the mayor, and I bet he was just waiting for the bank to open before going in. He'd empty out the safe-deposit box and no one would be the wiser, at least not until the real mayor wanted to add or remove something from it. But when Ellie blabbed our plans at the diner, he realized he had to lead us away from the bank first, so he left and returned looking like Elden. Elden told us he had a meeting on the mainland and that we should come talk to him tomorrow."

"Why were you going to talk to Elden?" Connor asked.

"We were curious about Adam's bragging in the bar. We were going to ask if it was justified based on what Herbert had in his accounts. We weren't going to ask for any specific information, just a little clue."

Connor looked at Adam. "So you're the one who broke into the mayor's house? He never noticed the key was missing. Adam Krawczyk, I'm adding the charge of breaking and entering to—"

Adam sat up. “No, that wasn’t me. That was my uncle. He stole the key, I only retrieved it from its hiding place. He was supposed to help me with all this, but instead he died.”

“All right then, he hid the key. That makes sense. It’s not smart to walk around with stolen property. Where did he hide it?”

Adam pressed his lips together until they turned white.

“He hid the key at the cottages, didn’t he?” I asked gently.

Adam said nothing, but the regret on his face told us everything we needed to know.

“You didn’t know which cottage, so you had to look through them all. Randy caught you and that’s when you shot him with Lulu’s gun.”

Adam put his head in his hands. “I didn’t mean to. I just wanted to get in and out, looking like Lulu. I wouldn’t have had to shoot him if she hadn’t called him while we were talking. He knew who I was and so I panicked. The gun was right there by the door and I shot him."

"Adam, you're under arrest for the murder of Randy Petit. For your own good, I urge you to get yourself a lawyer now."

Adam nodded. Through his sobs, he said, "I want a lawyer."

We left him in the interrogation room. "Such a complicated plan. He probably could have gotten away with it if he'd just walked away and tried again tomorrow," I said.

"He might have, but he was impatient and wanted money now."

The mayor was waiting for us in Connor's office. "You finally figured out what was stolen from my house. Can I have the key back?"

Connor took the key from the evidence bag and handed it to the mayor. "Out of curiosity, do you keep money or jewelry in the box?"

"No. Jewelry is in the safe at home, and my money is in various accounts at the bank. You can't earn interest, no matter how little it is, on anything in a box. I keep copies of important papers in the box."

I shook my head. All his scheming for nothing. And Randy? What did he see in the future that convinced him dying was the best alternative? We may never know.

CHAPTER 17

Jack gave me a few days off, and I spent them helping Marge with Randy's funeral arrangements. Yesterday, he had a beautiful service and then Marge, Ellie, and I took the mayor's boat out to sea to spread Randy's ashes. I invited Marge to come with me to Connor's for Thanksgiving today, but she said she wanted to be alone in Randy's house.

Ellie promised to check on her and bring her dinner, whether she wanted it or not.

Even though I'd been on the island for a year now, I hadn't stopped by to visit Connor's parents. I knew I'd made a terrible mistake choosing George over Connor, and I was embarrassed that twenty-year-old me wasn't able to see who did and didn't love me. His parents always thought Connor and I would marry and they insisted, from the time we were dating in high school, that I call them Mom and Dad.

Now I wasn't sure what to do. I felt like I'd let them down somehow, dashed their dreams for their future.

Ian told me not to bring anything because he had the menu completely sorted out. I couldn't arrive empty-handed, so I'd picked up a box of mixed chocolates from the combination flower and candy store. I clutched that box to me as though it were a shield that would ward off whatever disappointment his parents would relive by seeing me again.

I raised my hand to knock, but the door opened and Connor's father, a short balding man who favored flannel shirts and jeans—even on holidays—pulled me into an embrace.

"Rebecca! It's so good to see you again. Let me see you." He stood back and gave me an appraising look. "More beautiful than ever." He stepped aside and ushered me into the house.

The house had been updated since I'd been here last. The wood paneling, out of date even when it was up, had been replaced by white walls. Large, framed watercolors broke up the walls.

"Mother! She's here!" he yelled into the house.

Connor's mother rushed out of the kitchen and gave me an even larger hug. "It's so good to have you back, dear. Come sit with me and tell me everything. Connor won't tell us hardly anything—you know how he is."

"I . . . uh, thank you. The house looks lovely, Mrs.—"

She frowned at me for a brief second. "Oh no, we're not having any of that. We're still Mom and Dad to you, that is, unless you'd rather not."

I almost burst into tears right there. How could I not want to be a part of this family? I felt like these were the people I should be with, not my own parents who were often cold and reserved, and sometimes plain old mean.

"Okay, Mom." I handed her the box of chocolates. "These are for you."

The chocolates earned me another hug. "I won't be able to open them until tomorrow. Ian will have a fit if I change the flavor profile of the meal by adding anything."

"That's fine. I didn't dare bring a side dish for the same reason," I said.

Mom and Dad sat on the couch and I sat across from them in an overstuffed chair. "So, tell us everything, dear. We hear you have a daughter. I'm sure she's as beautiful as you are," Mom said.

I took my phone from my purse and pulled up the folder that contained all my photos of Kelsey. "Her name is Kelsey," I said as I handed my phone to them.

Mom and Dad started flipping through the photos, smiling and laughing at the goofy faces Kels had insisted on making when she was younger.

Connor came downstairs, his hair still wet from a shower. "Morning, sunshine," he said as he sat in the chair next to me.

"We're looking at photos of Kelsey. She's a lovely girl. Is she still in school?" Dad asked.

"She's at UC Berkeley. She's a physics major, but she plans to continue on to med school." I was grateful they didn't bring up George, or my divorce.

Although I thought I knew the answer, I couldn't help asking. "Should we be helping Ian at all? I can't cook like he does, but I could at least wash some dishes."

Mom almost jumped up with excitement. "He's already shooed me out of the kitchen twice, but you should come look at it. He had it completely renovated, and it's a dream to work in. And when he's not looking, we can snatch a bite of something."

"I heard that!" Ian yelled from the kitchen. "But you can come in for a minute."

The kitchen was much larger than I remembered it. "Did you expand the house to have a larger kitchen?" I asked.

Ian grinned. "We did. I've got enough room to work and mine and Connor's bedrooms are larger now too."

The oven timer went off. "Okay, everyone out. The turkey needs to come out, and I don't trust any of you not to pick at it before it's rested."

He opened the oven and pulled out a twenty-pound bird with crispy, golden skin. Once he set it down, he handed Connor a tray of mimosas and threatened to push us back into the living room. “Okay already,” Connor grumbled. “We get the picture.”

Connor handed us each a drink. “To a happy year full of love,” he toasted.

I took a sip and he put his arm around my waist, pulling me close.

This family was everything I’d ever wanted. I tried to create the warm, loving atmosphere for us and my in-laws, but they were as cold and reserved as George was. I shook my head and had another sip of mimosa. I was not going to waste any more time thinking about my ex. Not when I was spending the day with a family who loved me.

I set my glass down and walked to the doorway of the kitchen. Ian was busy assembling dishes and making what looked like two different kinds of gravy. “Are you sure I can’t help? Can I at least bring food out to the table?”

He looked around. "Not yet. Come back in fifteen minutes and I'll have something for you to do."

I went back to the living room and watched the end of the Thanksgiving Day parade. Before I knew it, and definitely before fifteen minutes was up, Ian called us into the dining room. The table and sideboard were loaded with food—the food I'd offered to help with. "You said you'd have something for me to do when I came back," I said.

He grinned. "I do. You need to sit and enjoy the meal."

I rolled my eyes. "Lame. I'm helping with the dishes, and I won't take no for an answer."

We sat and began passing food around the table. "So, Rebecca, I hear you were instrumental in catching the town's latest murderer," Mom said.

Connor glared at her. "She might not want to talk about it, you know. It was scary."

I patted his leg. “It was scary, but it’s over now so I can talk about it. But I’m surprised Connor didn’t tell you all about it.”

“Oh no,” Dad said, “he hardly ever talks about work. We learn more from the paper than we do from him.”

I thought about that for a moment and realized he did that on purpose. If he told them what kind of danger he was in on a regular basis, they’d worry far too much. “Well, it all started when Marge forced her Uncle Randy to hire me. The cottages were having some weird break-ins where nothing was stolen. He didn’t want to bother Connor with it, because it almost looked like there was no crime.”

“Pass the potatoes, Becks,” Connor said.

“I started looking into who might want something from the cottages, and later that day, Randy was killed. Suddenly I had a murder investigation on my hands.”

"You didn't want to give up? Your client was dead and the police were definitely involved then," Dad asked.

I shook my head and took the brussels sprouts from Ian. "He'd paid me a retainer and I at least needed to work enough to use it up. Besides, Randy helped me get out of some trouble when I was younger, and this was the last thing I could ever do to help him."

Mom nodded. "Of course you wanted to do right by him. He would have been proud of the way you solved this case."

I'd stopped by my parents' house yesterday to let them know I wasn't coming for dinner today. All they had to say about the case or the wildly flattering newspaper article about me was that it wasn't the kind of job they raised me to have and that if I kept dating Connor someday he'd get me killed.

Just when my mother and I had worked out a few of our differences, they came up with nonsense like that. I held back on telling them Connor and I would be happy to come for dessert because it had turned into a lie. Perhaps I'd talk to them at Christmas.

Then again, I might not. The Dougherty family was so happy to have me around, perhaps I'd do like I did in high school and spend as much time here as I could.

Dad chimed in. "We're very proud of you, Rebecca. Connor told me how you held onto Adam to try and keep him from running away. In the condition he left you in, honey, that takes an amazing amount of inner strength."

I tried to tell them anyone would have done what I did, but they refused to believe me. I begged for a change of subject and we moved on to the afternoon's football games. Connor's family had a long-standing tradition of betting the strangest things on the outcome of the games.

I bet Mom five hours of gardening work that the Giants would win over the Cowboys. I bet Dad an afternoon of fishing on his boat that the Vikings would win over the Patriots. He said this was blasphemy, but I said in a post-Brady era almost anything was possible. Finally I bet Ian a month of car washes that the Bills would win over the Lions. Other bets for the day included breakfast in bed for every weekend in December, a weekend trip to New York to see the ball drop for New Year's Eve, and after much brotherly prodding, Connor said that if the Lions won, he would move to the basement so that Ian could have a two-room bedroom suite upstairs.

When dinner was over, I forced my help on Ian. I packed the food up and put it away while he loaded the dishwasher. Connor snuck in and started washing the pots and pans. When we were done, Ian made coffee and we joined their parents in the living room for dessert.

I sipped my coffee and listened to this family that was proud of me, that loved me even though we weren't related, and finally felt like I'd come home again.

Thank you for reading Hormones, Homicides, and Hexes! I've planned several more cases for Rebecca and I can't wait to share them with you.

Until then, I think you'd love my Isabella Proctor Cozy Paranormal Mystery series. Check them out at bit.ly/LisaBouchard

Hormones, Homicides and Hexes

SNEAK PEEK

Leaf of Faith

Being a witch wasn't something we talked about with customers. It's been over four hundred years since my ancestor Elizabeth Proctor was convicted of witchcraft, and the fear of being found out still ran deep. That was why, on the surface, the witches in Portsmouth seemed like normal people. Okay, maybe not normal. Maybe harmlessly eccentric.

Take me, for example: I looked like any other twenty-one-year-old shopgirl with two jobs trying to make it on her own. I was five foot seven, and had black hair, dark blue eyes, and features that, to me, seemed too large for my face. My best friend, Abby, said I was glamorous, but I thought I was more of an ugly duckling. Abby has always been the beautiful one, with delicate features, gleaming golden hair, and the kind of grace and physical presence that resulted from over a decade of dance classes.

Maybe I wouldn't have stood out in a crowd, but I was one of the few potion witches in New Hampshire.

I grasped the ornate brass doorknob and pushed open the door to the Portsmouth Apothecary. The shop always smelled like the tea of the day, and today's was rose hip and hibiscus. I closed the door behind me and took a moment to survey the sales floor. The jars of herbs that lined the right-hand side of the shop were running low despite the stock we kept in the prep room, the candle display in the center of the room needed to be refilled, and several of the touristy knickknacks in front of the large picture window had been knocked off the table.

I quickly made my way to the office in the back where I hung up my coat and pulled my hair back into a bun. I loved this store and using my talents as a potion witch to help people—

human and witch—even if the humans didn't realize magic was involved.

Once I returned to the main room, I looked to Trina Bassett, my boss. Her lips were pinched in frustration and her left eye twitched. She was busy helping Mrs. Williams with an order. Mrs. Williams was in her seventies, but dressed and acted at least two decades younger. She was extremely particular and would choose each bud of lavender and chamomile for her tea blend. It took ages to complete her order every week. I could tell by the way Trina was holding her short, round body rigid that she was almost at the end of her patience.

"Good morning, Isabella," Trina called to me as she pulled a jar of lavender from its spot on the shelf and showed it to Mrs. Williams.

I smiled at her, hoping she'd read my encouragement. "Morning, Trina. Morning, Mrs. Williams."

Mrs. Williams pointed a bony finger to several lavender buds and Trina delicately pulled them out with a pair of tongs. Ordinarily, we use a scoop to remove the herbs from their jars, but not for Mrs. Williams. A half pound of tea might take an hour to assemble for her.

The clouds broke and sun flooded through the front window. The light reflected off the pale yellow walls, bathing the shop in a warm glow. March in New Hampshire was almost always gray, but these moments of sunshine reminded us better weather was coming. A glint of sunlight bouncing off a shard of broken glass near the herb jars caught my eye. I wanted to ask Trina what happened today that the shop was in such disarray, but that would have to wait until Mrs. Williams left. I grabbed the broom and dustpan from the closet by the back door. As I closed the closet door, Mrs. Williams raised her voice.

"I don't care what you think, Trina, you know the right thing to do, and I expect you to take care of it by tonight. I won't be held responsible if you don't."

Not wanting to intrude, I stood at the checkout counter in the back of the room. Once Mrs. Williams left, I swept the glass up while Trina replaced the flower jars she had been using. "What was that all about?" I asked.

"It's nothing to worry about, my dear," she said. Her grimace told me otherwise. I'd been Trina's apprentice for about a year, and she didn't hide her worry nearly as well as she thought she did.

I continued sweeping and found more shards of glass and sliced dong quai root. I picked the dong quai container off the counter to inspect it. It had been replaced by one of the new, wider jars Trina had been slowly changing to. Why had the old jar broken, and more importantly, why hadn't Trina cleaned it up completely?

Before I could ask, Trina handed me a glass vial. "Your investiture ceremony is coming up soon, right?"

"It's next week. Are you coming?"

"I wouldn't miss it for the world," Trina said.

Investiture was the time once every seven years that a witch chose what she would focus her work and study on. My cousins Thea and Delia and I would choose our first non-beginner focus. I planned to choose potions, and I didn't know what Thea or Delia would choose.

"In that case, it's time for a test. I'll finish tidying up. You have half an hour to tell me the eight components of this potion."

I blew hair out of my face and took the vial with me to my small counter in the prep room, across from the office. The small room had two counters, two chairs, and all our extra stock on shelves that lined three sides of the room. We kept the lights dim, because we stored photosensitive ingredients there.

Unlike the sales floor, the prep room smelled green and earthy. I sat in my chair, closed my eyes, and focused my mind. There was a standard method to determine potion ingredients, and as long as I worked through all the steps in the allotted time, I should be able to pass the test. I could cast a spell to determine the ingredients, but Trina was old-fashioned and wanted me to learn the non-magical methods I could use in front of customers. The first two tests were simple: smell and sight. I unstoppered the cork and immediately smelled pungent ginger oil. I poured the potion into a bowl and recognized the glimmer of pearl powder. Was this a longevity potion?

Before I moved to the next step, Trina opened the door. “Your mother called and said she needs you to call her right away.”

I was concentrating on my test and hadn't heard the phone ring. I rubbed my forehead. Anytime my mother had something she wanted to tell me, it was urgent—at least to her. I didn't want to interrupt my test for something that could wait for another twenty-five minutes.

"Did you tell her I was busy?"

"No, I didn't. Call her, and if you need a few more minutes to finish, you can have them. I'll be in the office if you need me."

I pulled my phone from my pocket and dialed. "Hi, Mom. I'm in the middle of a test. What's up?"

"Hi, sweetie, I know I said I wouldn't bother you when you moved out. It's been weeks since we've seen you, and we miss you," she said with a shaky voice.

I thought over the six months since I'd moved out and realized she was right. I'd planned on a slow withdrawal from daily family life when I moved out of the house to make the separation easier on everyone. I was the first person in two generations to move to an apartment, and my grandmother, mother, and aunts were all sad about my choice.

"Sorry about that. It's been incredibly busy and by the time I remember to call, it's too late at night."

"I need you to come to dinner tonight. I'm worried about your grandmother. Her health has taken a turn, and we can't figure out what is wrong," she said with more distress in her voice than I'd heard in a long time.

My heart sank. Grandma was seventy-seven, and although witches can live to twice that age, it wasn't guaranteed. "Sure, I can come for dinner, but how can I help?"

"Your grandmother listens to you, and I want you to convince her to see a doctor. Can you ask Trina to come by and have a look at her too?"

Grandma was stubbornly independent, thinking she knew enough herbal magic to keep herself alive almost forever. She started listening to my advice only once I'd become Trina's apprentice.

"I'm not sure she'll listen to me, but I'll give it a try."

"Good. Dinner is at six. Don't be late."

I hung up and turned to my potion, trying to put my worry about Grandma out of my mind.

"Is everything okay?" Trina asked from the doorway.

I looked up at her, willing myself to not cry. "Grandma's not well, and my mother and aunts can't figure out what's wrong. They want me to convince her to go see a doctor."

Trina shook her head. "Your grandmother's never seen a doctor in her life, I doubt she'll start going to one now."

"Can you come talk to her tonight?"

"I can't. I've got someone coming to the shop after hours. I have another idea. Leave the test vial here, and let's head out to the greenhouse."

I followed Trina out the back door and pulled my black cardigan tight against the cold March air. The rose and juniper bushes planted next to the greenhouse rustled in the wind. Our feet crunched on the gravel path that was finally devoid of snow.

The greenhouse was a small glassed-in building she had built in the shared courtyard behind the apothecary that provided most of the herbs and flowers we needed. The floor-to-ceiling shelves were full of rare and common plants we used in our tinctures, sold as dried goods, or ground into powder. I stepped in and took a deep breath. The oxygen-rich air, heady with the scent of early blooming roses and echinacea, cheered me. The bright flowers were a stark contrast to the dirty gray snow piled up along the edges of the courtyard and hinted at the change of season everyone longed for by the end of winter.

I'd learned a lot of gardening from my grandfather when I was younger, and I used his lessons to keep the greenhouse plants thriving. Grandpa and I spent our weekends year-round working on the family gardens: food, flower, memorial, and medicinal. If we weren't outside working in them during the warm months, we were by the fireplace in winter, planning changes and additions, or starting seeds in early spring.

Trina closed the door. "It's time for you to start using your powers to assemble potions. You've learned what each of these plants will do. Now you need to put that information together with what you know about other people to form an effective cure. You've been honing your intuition over the past year, and it's time to use it."

I stared at her, mouth open. “You want me to guess?”

She put her hand on my shoulder and gave it a reassuring squeeze. “No, I want you to think about someone you’re close to, someone you care about, and then let your instinct guide you.”

We stood silently for a moment while I thought.

“Who have you chosen?”

“Grandma,” I said.

Trina smiled. “I thought you’d pick her. Use your intuition and choose tincture, tea, or balm.”

“Tincture, because it will be easier to add to her food,” I said.

“Be wary, giving any medical assistance to someone without their permission is the first step in harming them and yourself.”

“I know.” It went deeper than that. Using magic on non-magical people was almost unilaterally frowned on. Healing potions were one of the very few exceptions, but even then, the person had to know the ingredients they were buying. There was no exception when the person being treated was a witch.

"Close your eyes and focus on your grandmother. Once you have her in mind, allow your intuition to guide you to the plants she needs. Once you have identified each one, we'll go inside and you will make the tincture."

I bit my lip and closed my eyes. Once I had Grandma firmly in mind, the lemon tree, the rosemary bush, and the small juniper bush outside the greenhouse took her place in my vision. I opened my eyes. "Lemon, juniper and rosemary."

Trina nodded. "Okay then, pick a little of each and meet me inside."

When I returned to the prep room, I put the tincture ingredients on my table and looked into the office, where Trina was on her cell phone with her back to me.

Her shoulders stiffened. "Where do you think I'm going to get that kind of money?"

A man was yelling on the other end of the line, but I didn't recognize his voice. It could have been anyone, because the phone made his voice sound tinny.

"I don't care where you get it, or what you need to do to get it. I'm coming today and you don't want to disappoint me."

LEAF OF FAITH is available now!

Find out what Trina's talking about, and what's wrong with Grandma Esther in Leaf of Faith. You can find it at bit.ly/LisaBouchard

ABOUT THE AUTHOR

It all started when she learned to read at five. One of her first and favorite memories is of words taped to all the objects in the house. Not long after that, books became the best thing ever and there was no turning back.

She suffered a crisis of confidence in High School and College and decided writing was too difficult, so she earned a degree in Chemistry and later enrolled in a Physics PhD program instead. Three career changes and four children later, she's back to writing and much happier for it.

Now she works from her home office in New Hampshire amid the books, kids, and occasional pets.

Learn more about Lisa and her books, and be sure to sign up for her newsletter at www.LisaBouchard.com

North of Forty

Rebecca Wright has finally had enough. Enough of her cheating husband, enough of molding herself into the image he thinks she should present, and enough of their shallow city life. When she becomes telepathic in midlife, she knows it's all got to change. Follow her as she moves back to the town she loves and starts her life over as a private investigator. Cases should be easy to solve with telepathy, right? Not when people lie to themselves as much as other people.

Isabella Proctor Cozy Paranormal Mysteries

Follow Isabella, a spirited young witch, as she blossoms into her power and safeguards her town. Alongside Detective Palmer and her sassy talking cat Jameson, she uncovers mysteries and combats supernatural threats. A captivating blend of humor, heart, and whimsy weaves magical escapades that resonate with fans of paranormal and cozy mysteries alike. Join Isabella as she navigates friendships, family, love, and the spellbinding world of magic.